Tuesday, January 12th, 2016 – Present day – 12:13am

The sound of sirens fills the downtown area of Gullburg. A herd of cop cars and fire trucks head toward one of the biggest fires the town has ever seen. The authorities arrive at the same moment as a pack of cars, full of concerned parents and siblings. The air is full with the smell of ash and a musky scent. It is difficult to breathe, and even harder to see. The warehouse is coming down in pieces. It is rumored there were about a hundred kids at a party in the warehouse when the fire started accidentally. No one is giving any answers, and civilians are starting to riot. The commotion comes to a halt when a few students inform the authorities that one from the bunch is missing, and has not been seen since he became sick inside the warehouse bathroom. The explosion in the warehouse had the potential to incinerate bodies, according to the authorities. The questions for the police come in a violent wave, and the citizens of Gullburg are beginning to lose patience.

1

Chapter I

Family Ties

December 25, 2005, 6:47am – 11 years ago

The sun rises above the beaten down town. The thin layer of snow on the ground glows. The streets are silent. Inside the houses, children rush downstairs to their Christmas trees. In the Jameson residence at 413 Dupe Lane, twins Kyle and Amy Jameson, age seven, are on their way downstairs. Kyle rushes down the stairs in attempt to beat Amy, chanting "First one down opens first!" Amy chuckles while attempting to squeeze past Kyle. They reach the tree and eagerly await their parents, so they can dig into their presents.

"You may have won, but you know my gifts will be better," Amy says playfully.

Kyle smiles at Amy. They yell for their parents to come downstairs as fast as they can.

Mr. Jameson shouts down to the children, "Alright, alright, you pack of wolves, we're coming! We're coming!"

Mr. and Mrs. Jameson approach the bottom of the steps, both yawning, both with bags under their eyes. Amy and Kyle fidget with excitement until their parents motion to start unwrapping. Not a second passes before both of the twins are into the gifts, strewing wrapping paper everywhere; looking like it went through a shredder. Kyle opens his first gift, chosen even though it's not the biggest or most appealing box. He reaches inside the gift wrap to find a keychain necklace.

On the necklace is a charm of a baby ox. Kyle stares at the gift with curiosity, and some confusion, but the baby ox holds his attention despite the fact that it isn't a toy.

Mr. Jameson notices Kyle and calls out, "Who is that from, pal?"

Kyle flips back to the tag which reads *Amy*. He tells his father that it's from his sister. Amy smiles cheek to cheek and raises her arm in the air. Mr. and Mrs. Jameson's eyes meet, and they smile in unison.

"Now that's not just a keychain of a bull, you know that? You know what that is? Don't you remember, son?"

Images play in Kyle's mind and he remembers, but can't get it out before Amy shouts "Peter, St Peter! It's that keychain grandma gave me."

Now Kyle realizes what the charm is, and he thinks back to the prayers their Grandma used to say when she put them to bed. Kyle's face is flushed with a look of appreciation, but asks Amy why she is giving him such a special charm; this was their Grandma's last gift to her. Amy hugs Kyle, and he squeezes her even tighter. Amy whispers, "So you know, I will always have your back."

Kyle pulls away. The look on his face is so touching that it floods Amy with thankfulness. He puts the necklace around his neck. The Jamesons watch their children with joy, and hug one another as the kids begin to open the remaining presents.

The roar of pointless chatter, curse words and insults fly like arrows in every direction as the Gullburg High School cafeteria is swarmed for lunch period. The room is small but adequate and is full of tables with narrow aisles that seem only inches wide. Kyle enters and walks toward his table, accompanied by Amy and their friends Spencer, Jamie, Connor, and Amy's boyfriend, Mark.

Spencer – your stereotypical rebel – gets the table's attention by posing the question, "So, who's going to the party tonight?"

Kyle has grown up being far from the biggest party animal. He responds to Spencer in a very condescending and sarcastic manner, asking Spencer if he is referring to his animal, papier-mâché art sculpture art final.

Everyone laughs and Spencer rolls his eyes at Kyle. "Don't make me hit you man."

Kyle smirks and continues eating.

Amy, who is still giggling to herself, mutters, "Come on Spence. You know Kyle's determined to graduate so he can be broke." She laughs again.

Mark – your everyday, burly, jock type – laughs at Spencer and Amy's comments, and at Kyle. "In poverty for life with that profession, ha-ha." Unlike Kyle, Mark is the complete party animal package; he does not have a 'five year plan', so to speak. Kyle looks up from his food and his sketches with a proud look of accomplishment on his face. He refutes Mark's comment.

Kyle informs the entire table that Amy and Mark will attend different universities next year, and Mark will cheat on his sister within sixty seconds of coming in contact with any female. He finishes his aggressive statement with a question: "Isn't that how it happened at Angelina's party, Mark? Or was that thirty seconds?"

The vibe of the table is completely shattered, as if a huge glass pitcher has been dropped on it. The room is dead silent. Everyone's eyes are locked on Kyle and Mark.

Mark immediately lunges out of his seat towards Kyle, and Kyle shows no fear, not moving an inch. Spencer intercepts Mark and grabs him by the arm.

Spencer leans in and slowly whispers, "Mark, everyone at the table makes jokes at Kyle's expense. It's about time he rebutted. Plus, we both know I could tell Amy much worse about you and other girls."

Spencer leans away, shooting Mark a look of pure victory and domination. Mark just nods and makes a beeline for the exit.

As Spencer sits down Connor breaks the silence. "Glad they are finally getting along."

Jamie and Kyle chuckle, but they see the look of embarrassment and disgust on Amy's face. Kyle knows this is going to be one of those days. The mood has become awkward and silent.

Amy's jaw opens as if a *three-two-one* countdown to a race has been called. "I am so done with you Kyle!" she shouts. "Stop saying things you don't know to be true, especially when they have to do with my relationship. You are being so selfish. Just because you're a loner and can't connect with anyone who possesses a pulse, does not mean you get to make up damaging lies about my relationship."

She storms out after Mark as soon as she has finished her speech. Kyle, shockingly, looks a bit bummed, as if he actually feels bad. Jamie pats him on the back and reassures him that they all know what kind of guy Mark is, and that they know Kyle just wants the best for Amy. Connor and Spencer nod in unison and Spencer announces that Amy will find out the 'hard way' – which is Kyle's concern.

Due to recent stressful events, Kyle informs the group, he will be going to that party tonight.

Spencer chants loud enough for the whole room to hear his excitement, "Kyle is finally leaving his bedroom at night!"

People at a bunch of tables quietly clap at the far end of the cafeteria. Kyle cannot help but smile. He has to admit that this outing is overdue, and he is eager to get out. "Connor, Jamie, you guys are going, right?

Jamie nods. "Absolutely we are!"

The school day comes to an end as the sound of the horrible 40-year-old bell fills the halls, rattling off each wall and locker. The swarm of eager students race to exit the building on the last Thursday before winter break. Kyle takes his time at his locker and avoids the mosh pit of students at the exit. He hasn't seen Amy or Mark since lunch. However, since a bad day usually ends with Mark confronting Kyle at his locker, maybe this is for the best.

Spencer creeps up behind Kyle and slams his locker shut before Kyle can grab another book. Kyle smirks at Spencer and heads out with him.

"No extra work for you tonight my man. Nope, no way", Spencer shouts.

Kyle tries to reason with him. "I know, I know. The party, me going, I get the picture" He laughs.

"That's damn right," Spencer says, with the sparkle of excitement and poor teenage decision-making in his eyes.

They head out of school behind the crowd and make their way in the direction of Spencer's house. Kyle continues past the turn to his house. Spencer looks at him in confusion and asks him what his plan is. Kyle gives him a very distinct stare that Spencer recognizes.

"I am going to stay for TWO – just two – games of Mortal Kombat, Spence."

Spencer laughs. He proceeds to inform Kyle that it is impossible, due to the fact it takes Kyle at least three games to beat him. Kyle finds Spencer's comment comical and reciprocates with some laughter. He assures Spencer that he won't be staying long since he must get home at a reasonable time to start his art final.

Spencer doesn't argue, since he wants Kyle to go to the warehouse party tonight. Kyle says he doesn't want to intrude on Spencer's dinner when his folks get home. He notices Spencer's silence and his shrug of annoyance and inquires as to what is wrong.

10

Spencer neglected to inform Kyle that his parents are splitting up for a little while.

"Our tiny place wasn't worth the hassle since they don't love each other anymore; splitting up was the easiest decision."

There is a very uncomfortable vibe followed by a moment of silence between the two. Kyle finally musters up some words and pats Spencer on the back, apologizing, and assures Spencer that if he needs anything, all he has to do is ask.

"Thanks man, but it's totally screwed. My dad lost his job for suing a hospital. The hospital stole a research article from him and plagiarized his work. Having no money just caused too many fights. My mom has been working double shifts at the diner, and my dad skipped town, he was so upset. He couldn't stand to be in this town anymore, he was totally broken."

Again unable to find the right words to say to comfort his friend, Kyle nods and tells Spencer he will see him later that evening.

Kyle heads home to get a jump on his work for next day, remembering that his parents want to have dinner as a family tonight. However, considering his last encounter with Amy, he decides that he is not so eager to arrive home. He decides to stop in at a small tavern that rarely cards minors.

The doorway is empty, and there is an open lane to the bar. Upon Kyle's arrival, the bartender neglects to ask for any form of ID. Kyle orders a draft, and peers up at the news on the TV above him. He notices a worn-down woman from across the bar. She hasn't taken her eyes off of him since he walked through the door. He feels uncomfortable and wonders about this lady's intentions, uncertain if she is unbalanced or simply interested in speaking to him. She stands up slowly, and Kyle notices a distinct limp in her right leg. She makes eye contact with him, pays her tab, walks toward the door, and leaves.

A few minutes pass while Kyle finishes his beer. Before he stands up to leave, the bartender pours a gin and tonic for him and walks away. Kyle calls out to inform her that there must have been be some mistake; he didn't order the drink. The bartender whispers, "I know, the lady who left a bit ago did, sweetie."

Kyle is confused but downs the free drink, then heads for home.

He walks through his front door, and tosses the last of his mints in his mouth. He figures dinner will be unpleasant enough, even without his parents all over him for drinking – surely Amy has shared with them the incident at lunch. Kyle drops his bag in the living room and enters the kitchen, awaiting the scolding session that he is certain will soon commence. That last free drink from the ever-so-creepy mystery woman is on Kyle's mind. Despite the rattle in his head, he pulls it together, quietly sitting with his parents and Amy. Dinner is a very quiet affair. As they all fill their plates not a word is spoken. Mr. and Mrs. Jameson share a look – a sort of marital telepathy.

Mr. Jameson wonders out loud, "So whose turn is it to ask them what's going?"

Mrs. Jameson signals that he should be the one to ask.

Mr. Jameson says, "So am I going to sit here and pretend that you two are all happy-go-lucky all night, or is one of you going to share with us what's going on?"

The question is not followed by a response. Kyle and Amy continue to stare down at their plates, ignoring each other.

Mrs. Jameson looks at Amy as if to insist that she open her mouth and give them some answers.

Amy rolls her eyes. "Well, not much can go right when my brother insists he knows more about my relationship then I do…"

Kyle quickly cuts her off, contributing his opinion that maybe Amy wouldn't have communication issues if she didn't ignore the facts about Mark.

"Oh my god Kyle, screw you and your Picasso lonely self," Amy replies loudly.

"Okay," Mr. Jameson interjects. "Enough!"

Both parents inform them that if something doesn't change, their lives are about to become more complicated. "Come on

14

children, when you are about to head out to college, this is when you need each other most." Mr. Jameson says.

Kyle shrugs, stands up and walks toward the door. Mr. and Mrs. Jameson both ask where he is going. Kyle shares his plans for the evening: Amy and Mark overly stressed him out today, so he told Spencer that he would go to a party with him.

"You never head out on weeknights, Kyle," Mrs. Jameson says. "Also, I thought you had that art final to finish?"

Kyle assures her that he intends to finish his art final, but he needs a breather. "Well, Mom and Dad, it's been a long day, and like you said, college is soon. I'm not going to let worthless people ruin my last few months; I'll be home whenever Princess can come get me."

Amy's eyes open wide in alarm. "Umm no, I have plans with Mark later. I can't come pick you up."

"Shocker," Kyle responds.

Mr. Jameson intervenes and suggests to Amy that it wouldn't kill her to skip one night with Mark to help her brother who never goes out.

Amy jumps up from the table and storms off, knocking her plate to the ground as food spills everywhere. "Fine, go ahead and spoil Kyle. Fine by me!" she says as she slams the door. The vase on the mantel shakes, almost falling over.

Mr. and Mrs. Jameson are not exactly pleased with the outcome of this dinner, but they know complaining will not solve their little dilemma. This has to be done in baby steps. Kyle and Amy won't start to get along overnight. Mrs. Jameson reassures Kyle that he will not be stranded, and promises that Amy will pick him up by the end of the night.

Kyle thanks her as he throws on his jacket and heads out. Mr. Jameson gives Kyle ten bucks and whispers, "Have a fun night, but please be careful, son."

As he frantically searches the nearby rooms for his shoes, Kyle assures his dad that he will be.

16

Kyle received his third call from Spencer, who is waiting outside in his car, and Kyle continues searching as fast as he can, while texting Spencer that he will be right out.

Outside, Spencer reads the texts, turns his music up and patiently waits for his friend. Spencer's car seat starts to vibrate as he receives a call. He reaches around for his phone. As he locates it he sees that "Amy Jameson" is calling him. For a second he is hesitant to answer. He picks up on one of its final rings.

"What is it, Amy?"

"I need a favor and you're going to have to be the one to help me."

"What could you possibly need? And what makes you think I have any interest in helping you?"

"Well, what I need is for you to get Kyle drunk enough that I don't need to come get him tonight. I don't care how you do it, just get it done. As for why you would help, I am sure you'd like to keep what happened at our lake house last summer a secret from Kyle. Wouldn't you?"

Spencer gave a deep sigh. "You are such a bitch, Amy. There is not one good thing about you. However, I don't want to lose my best friend so sure… I'll be your puppet tonight."

"That's what I thought. I'll be with Mark. I won't be showing up. Just get it done."

Spencer slams his phone down on his dashboard and punched the passenger seat.

Kyle runs out from the front door and approaches the car. Spencer grabs his phone, puts the music back on, and adopts a happy face. "You ready for a night you'll never forget, big guy?"

Kyle laughs and asks Spencer if he is going to regret going tonight. Spencer assures him that he'll have fun, and that he needs it with all the bullshit going on with him, Mark, and his sister. Kyle agrees.

Spencer starts the ignition and they head down the wet, dimly lit street. They arrive at the old Gullburg sneaker warehouse, where all the seniors have held their parties for years.

Spencer kills the engine, then jumps out of his seat and slams the car door. "Ahhhh! Now it is time to get stuff going, my man!" He winks at Kyle. Together, they head toward the entrance.

Kyle finds himself holding Spencer's case of beer, and Spencer begins ripping into the box before they enter the building. Spencer grabs a second beer out of the box and tosses it to Kyle. Kyle, who is stumbling to hold the case and catch the beer Spencer threw at him, finds a corner to hide the box.

They move through the crowd, searching for Connor and Jamie, but locating them is difficult. There are more students from their high school than would fit comfortably in the room. Spencer signals to Kyle that he is going to go to the bathroom, and then disappears into the crowd. Kyle sips his beer and looks around for their friends.

"Kyle! Kyle! Over here!" Connor yells from the ping pong table across the room.

Kyle spins around to locate Connor. He spots Jamie waving her arm in the air. Kyle walks over to the table where Connor and

19

Jamie are playing drinking games with a group of cheerleaders. Initially Kyle is hesitant to continue drinking, but thanks to Jamie he becomes enamored with various beer ball games.

Jamie wants Kyle to have a good night. She feels for him, and always seems to be the one who understands how he is feeling.

"I don't think I am going to help the team much," Kyle says, "I'm not known for my beer ball skills."

Jamie chuckles and strokes Kyle's arm, assuring him that it doesn't matter, and that they're all just happy he's there tonight. The team of Kyle, Jamie, and Connor lose the first game.

Spencer approaches from the far side of the room. He slurs his words as he yells, "Now how did y'all go and lose like that? Alright, restart. I'm in this time. Let's go, guys."

The three of them laugh and roll their eyes, and set up the table for the rematch. Spencer continues to mess with Kyle. He tells him if they lose he has to take a shot, and if they win he has to take two. Kyle rolls his eyes and laughs as he informs his friends that he may just have to lose on purpose now.

Connor cuts them off. "Okay! Okay! Enough talk. Let's get this going, guys!"

The four of them line up. Spencer calls out, "Ready, set, drink!" Both sides immediately start chugging their beers. Kyle is the last of the four to go, so if they are losing, it'll be up to him to pull the weight. Kyle notices that Jamie is slowing down and their team is falling behind.

He takes a deep breath as his turn approaches. He is only just beginning to chug his beer as his opponent is nearly halfway done. Kyle opens his throat, jolts his head back, and the entire beer slides down his throat like a kid going down a water slide. He slams his cup down and cries out, "And done!"

The whole room erupts in applause and chants. Spencer and Jamie's faces show utter disbelief. They could not be happier to be so shocked; they start throwing high fives at Kyle, while thanking him for putting their team on his back. Kyle is overwhelmed by all the cheers and congratulations. He is smiling broadly, and realizes that he is having a great time.

"Hell yeah. Kyle!" Spencer shouts. However, he does not forget what he has to do for Amy.

Kyle is not drinking at a pace to pass out before needing a ride home. Spencer was prepared for this, and so he brought a few of his mom's sleeping pills from her medicine cabinet. He crushes a pill into one of Kyle's two shots and hands them to him. Kyle smiles and takes them happily. Jamie and Connor grab theirs as well, and they all down them together on the count of three. They all squint due to the sour, brutal taste of the knock-off fifteen-dollar bottle of tequila, courtesy of Spencer. Once they all manage to get the shots down, and get the nasty taste out of their mouths, they gather closer together for a group picture to capture the night Kyle actually left his bedroom. Kyle tells them how much he appreciates them pushing him to have a fun night, especially with graduation approaching. In unison, they respond to his thanks, assuring him they will always have his best interests at heart. Graduation will only be the beginning of their lifelong friendship. Kyle is touched, and they exchange a group hug. Kyle heads off to the bathroom and says he will meet them back at the game table.

Spencer goes to the entrance where Kyle dropped off his case of beer, and he brings it to the back for all of them to share. Connor grabs one and heads to the bathroom as well. Connor ducks into the first stall and sees Kyle's shoes on the ground, as if he is on his knees in the stall next to him.

He knocks gently. "Kyle...Kyle are you good? It's Connor."

Kyle grunts. Barely making any sense, and bumps the stall door open for Connor to enter. Kyle has his head face down in the toilet, puking viciously.

Connor asks Kyle if he's okay. Kyle nods his head, and gives him a thumbs-up as he sends another batch of puke down the toilet. Connor laughingly tells Kyle he will go get him water and be right back. He heads back to Spencer and Jamie to tell them what he has discovered.

"Oh, of course Kyle's sick," Spencer says with a chuckle. "That's what the poor guy gets for not drinking his whole high school career."

"Come on, guys. Someone needs to go help him," Jamie says with a hint of annoyance in her voice.

Rolling his eyes, Spencer accepts the task, and grabs a bottle of water and heads to the bathroom. Kyle has yet to move an inch. Spencer arrives to give him the water, and sets his phone down on the floor beside Kyle, and helps him get the water down.

"You're going to be alright, man. I have a girl lined up that I want to go make some moves on."

Kyle struggles to get words out. He mumbles that it's okay and for Spencer to go ahead and not worry about him. Spencer rushes out of the bathroom and looks back around the party for the friend of Jamie's that he was making progress with.

When Spencer finally discovers Jamie and her friend, they are in a panic, as is the rest of the party.

"What? What is it? Is it cops? Are they busting us?"

Jamie's face is as white as the game table. She points to the flames at the corner of the room. The air smells of gas.

Spencer's eyes grow wide. He and Connor join the crowd of kids running and screaming out of the building. Everyone fights their way out of the crowded entrance as fast as they can.

The buildings walls begin to collapse as police and fire trucks speed towards the warehouse. Just as the final wave of students sprint out of the warehouse, the building begins to blow to the sky, floor by floor. Walls, banisters, and pieces of doors start to come down in every direction.

The lights and flames fill the night sky like fireworks. In the moment of panic and fear when they ran from the building, Spencer, Jamie, and Connor gave no thought to the fact that Kyle was still in the bathroom as all of this was happening. They realize this as the explosion continues, and they scream out for help, trying to run back in to save Kyle.

The police tackle Connor as he heads towards the building. "No! No!" he shouts. "You don't understand! Our friend! Our friend he is in there! He's in there! Kyle!"

The building gives off its final explosive collapse, and it falls to the ground. Parents approach on the other side of the tape labeled *Caution*. Amy gets out of her car and runs to her parents to see what is going on. The Jameson family has yet to be informed that Kyle is unaccounted for, and they are overwhelmed with fear and worry for their son.

Amy pushes through the crowd as her parents attempt to get answers from the authorities. She finds Jamie and Spencer.

"Guys! Oh my God! Thank God you guys are okay. What happened? Where's Kyle?"

Spencer's and Jamie's eyes are full of tears, and their faces grow long. Amy asks again where Kyle is, and what's going on.

Spencer musters up the strength to compose himself. He informs Amy that Kyle had passed out in the bathroom and he didn't make it out of the warehouse. They don't know where Kyle is, but by the look of the warehouse, there was no realistic chance that Kyle survived.

Amy falls to her knees, staring at what is left of the warehouse. She is in shock, and can't even conjure up enough strength to cry. Amy makes eye contact with her parents, as she sees a police officer informing them of what has happened. Mr. and Mrs. Jameson are in agony.

Mr. Jameson hugs his wife, who is crying out in pain for her son. Amy looks back toward the building, feeling nothing but guilt. She makes eye contact with Spencer. With only a look, she is asking Spencer if this is their fault. Spencer nods and looks to the ground in disgust, as Jamie hangs onto him, crying...

The sirens quiet, and the commotion starts to end. For most families, this is a moment of thanks and relief, a time to count their blessings. However, for the Jamesons, and for Kyle's friends, this is the beginning of pain and suffering, a night they will never, ever be able to forget...

Chapter II

Goodbye

Obituaries

Kyle Patrick Jameson

Kyle Patrick Jameson, age 18, son of Alex and Marie Jameson, and sibling twin of Amy Jameson. Kyle was planning to go to college to study art and design, and was a senior at Gullburg High School. Kyle passed away late Thursday night in an accidental warehouse fire. The Jamesons will be holding a small service for Kyle this Sunday, January 17, at 1:00pm. Everyone is welcome, *as we celebrate Kyle with a beautiful*

and peaceful service. He will be dearly

missed.

Two weeks have passed since the horrid accident at the warehouse. The Jamesons and the whole town of Gullburg are still suffering from the loss of their beloved Kyle. A light snow drifts down from above, but does not lie on the ground. It feels like Christmas, but the beauty of Christmas is lacking. The Jamesons get out of their car as Spencer, Connor, and the graveyard assistants lift the marble-white casket out of the black funeral coach. Amy and her mom weep, tears streaming down their faces. Amy looks out into the distance. She needs a second with her eyes away from her brother's casket.

She catches a glimpse of someone maybe fifty yards away, a woman peering over the hill, listening to the service. Amy looks down for a moment, and when she looks up she sees the figure limp towards a car. Mr. Jameson hugs them both from behind, and they walk behind the casket, the crowd following behind. The casket is set on the lowering device but is not yet lowered.

The minister steps up to the podium and waits for the crowd to gather around and settle. The crowd stops talking but there are still occasional cries and whimpers. The minister rises up to the podium, which holds Kyle's senior photo.

"Today we gather, to mourn the loss of one of our loved ones, someone dear to us, one who will be in all of hearts, forever. The world may have taken Kyle from us physically, but we will never truly be without him."

The minister pauses for the crowd to say their prayers. Amy can barely comprehend that this is now reality.

"Kyle is with us today, he will be with us tomorrow, and for years to come. Kyle was one who always cared for others. He cared for them before himself and, more importantly, he even cared for those who he barely knew. Not everyone is as blessed to have someone like Kyle in their lives, but we were that lucky. We take this day as a remembrance of Kyle and all the joy he brought to us and this town. He will be with us until the end, and now... I ask that we take a moment of silence in honor of Kyle."

The crowd shares this moment of silence, which feels like an eternity, as the casket is lowered into the ground. Amy cries inconsolably. Her father holds her and she hides her face in his chest to mask the sadness. Spencer, Jamie, and Connor huddle together as they mourn the loss of their friend. Kyle's casket reaches the bottom and the casket is released from the lowering device.

The crowd starts to disperse. Mr. and Mrs. Jameson start to head toward the car, while Amy stays behind for a moment to say her goodbyes to her twin brother. She feels alone, and completely responsible for this accident.

Someone gives Amy a comforting rub from behind. She turns to see Spencer there, with the same look of regret on his face.

"How is this happening, Spence? I just wanted to stay out for a night... I know that Kyle and I fought, but could this…" Her tears overwhelm her, and she turns and hugs Spencer. Spencer continues to comfort Amy and stares down at the grave. He turns Amy towards the parking lot and they slowly walk away.

A few months have passed since the funeral and the town is finally starting to return back to normal. Everyone works to get on with their everyday lives. The students all gather for their annual Valentine's Day Date Dance that is held in the cheap, knock-off hotel downtown. This ballroom is a poorly constructed room, clearly not up to code, with poor air conditioning. The school has a meager budget for school sponsored events, but the students are just happy with someplace to go. The lights are dim and the DJ plays the fast-paced pop music. Amy sits in her chair by the refreshment table. She is obviously not getting back on with her life as quickly, or easily as the rest of the town.

Jamie and Connor leave the dance floor and make their way toward Amy to try and brighten her night, and get her mind off things.

"Hey Am! How's your night? Why don't you come and dance with us?" Jamie says emphatically.

"I'm okay here, but thank you guys. Really I know you're just trying to cheer me up. I appreciate it." Amy says.

Jamie and Connor sigh and exchange defeated looks. They express to Amy that they don't expect her to be back to normal, but she needs to try to keep her mind off of things.

Amy agrees and acknowledges that they are right, but still insists she is okay just hanging at the table. "I may catch up with you guys soon, okay?"

Jamie smiles and nods at Amy, and she and Connor head back toward the crowd of students.

Amy stares at the crowd. A part of her wishes she could go out there, but she is just not ready yet. She twirls her straw and stares at her soda.

Spencer runs out of the bathroom with a powerful skip in his step and makes his way towards Amy. "Hey, how are you doing? Why are you still just hiding all alone over here?"

Amy looks at Spencer condescendingly. "Does that question really require an answer, Spence?"

Spencer implores Amy to snap out of it and just try to enjoy herself; he insists it may even help her recovery process.

"Not everyone can cope as easily as you, and I know I certainly don't have the help that you do."

Spencer shrugs and partially ignores Amy's remark, insisting he has no idea what she means.

"Oh come on, Spencer, I know you, I have known you for a while, and they aren't serving powdered donuts tonight so I doubt that's what you were shoving in your face..."

Spencer wipes his nose. "Okay. So sue me, Amy. This is how I cope. Today marks two months since Kyle passed. It's not hurting you or anyone else, just hurting me. As far as I'm concerned this is the bare minimum of what I deserve for what we did. Don't judge me until you can accept that burden as well. Maybe socialize or something, anyone who knows the truth won't feel bad for you."

Spencer tosses his chair away and storms off. With tears in her eye, Amy storms toward the dance floor to find Jamie and Connor. She works her way through the crowd, and finally sees her friends in the middle of the floor.

As approaches, Jamie shouts, "Am!" Their faces fill with excitement as they welcome Amy back to the wonderful world of socializing.

Amy rolls her eyes and smiles at the both of them, and begins to dance. A large football player from Jefferson who came as someone's date dances into Jamie, knocking her over. He offers no apology. This angers the three of them. They help Jamie back to her feet. Connor approaches the football player with every intention of demanding an apology. Amy stops him, insisting he isn't worth the effort.

The DJ jumps off the stage and makes his way toward the jock. Amy, Jamie and Connor notice this and sit back to see what happens. The DJ grabs the jock's arm roughly and suggests he apologize to the girl he just put on the ground.

"Oh and who the hell are you, huh pal?"

The DJ lets his arm go and insists in a polite manner that he apologize to her.

The jock laughs and tells him to walk away while he still can.

"Listen man, I don't want a problem, but you knocked the poor girl over, you're going to have to let her know you didn't mean it."

The jock pushes the DJ back a few feet and moves toward him with fists out. Jamie jumps in front and he pulls back his arm.

"He didn't push me over – you did. All he is accountable for is being a decent human being, so get the hell away from us."

The jock slowly backs away laughing, grabs his date's waist and disappears into the crowd. Jamie turns to the DJ and hugs him, ambushing him with thanks.

"It's no problem, really," he replies. "I never liked guys like that when I was in high school, and they usually just stole my girlfriend. So it's really no problem. In this instance, he just lacked basic manners."

Jamie pulls away from her emotional hug and smiles. "Well, regardless, you have no idea who I am and you came out of your way to help me, so thank you." She leans in and kisses the DJ on the cheek.

Amy and Connor feel a bit awkward just standing there. Connor breaks the silence by asking him how long he has been a DJ.

He tells the kids he graduated from a high school about thirty minutes south of them. He finished school two years ago, and has been DJing to pay the bills after his parents kicked him out of the house. The group sympathizes with him and thanks him again for helping them.

"Well I would never kick you out of my house, and I would also like to show you around mine..." Jamie takes the DJ's hand and writes her number down on it. Amy stares at Jamie wide-eyed, unsure if that was a good idea.

Connor once again breaks the silence and asks the DJ, "So before we all head out, I never caught your name, man. So sorry — what was it?" He reaches out to shake his hand.

"It's Zach," he says as he pulls away from the handshake.

Jamie waves back at him and winks as they leave the dance floor crowd and head toward the ball room.

"Well, what an interesting night," Amy mutters.

Connor shakes his head in amazement. "Yeah, I guess we're just lucky Spencer wasn't there. He would have caused a massive scene with that asshole."

Jamie asks where Spencer went off to anyway. Amy tells them that she and Spencer got into a little argument and he left a while ago. Connor asks Amy what happened.

"It was just Spencer being Spencer," Amy says condescendingly, "and me yelling about his drugs – the usual. He'll be fine in an hour." The group laughs in unison, acknowledging how true that is. They grab their coats and head out to the car and go home.

The next day Amy wakes up quite late, well past noon. She gets her day started and looks for an outfit for dinner tonight with Mark. She heads to the bathroom to shower, leaving her phone on her bedside dresser. She turns on the water to warm it up and comes back out to gather a change of clothes for lunch, looking through her closet and trying to decide what to wear.

She hears her phone vibrate and buzz from the other side of the room. The phone vibrates again before she gets over to it. She reaches for her phone to see who messaged her. However, it wasn't a text at all. She has received a message from her online English homework website. This strikes Amy as odd, considering that it is Sunday. She opens the message and her jaw drops along with the phone. She jolts her foot up so the phone doesn't crush her toe and stumbles back onto the bathroom floor.

Barely breathing, Amy stares at her phone on the carpet a few feet away and slowly crawls back over to it. She reaches out again for the phone and double checks the notification: *Is there any homework this weekend?* The issue of homework doesn't upset Amy. What really strikes her is what is written above the message. *From: Kyle, Seat 9B.*

She throws her phone back onto the bed with a fit of rage. She figures this is Spencer, and that this is payback for last night. Amy has reached her limit – she is done with Spencer and his ridiculous, disgusting humor.

Later that night, Amy meets up with Mark for their two-year anniversary dinner. Amy's mind is elsewhere, but she attempts to keep that hidden from Mark. They approach the table at the small Italian restaurant where they had their first date. Mark pulls the chair out for Amy and then sits down to look at the menu. He soon looks up from his menu; he already knows what he wants, since nothing has changed in the intervening two years.

"Two years seems like it went by so fast, Am."

Amy twirls her hair and sips the water slowly from her straw. She nods in agreement.

Mark notices Amy's disinterest and asks what's wrong. "Am... Amy?"

Amy shoots her head up as if she has snapped out of a trance. "Yeah, sorry – what were you saying, babe?"

Mark, with a look of frustration on his face, takes a deep breath before responding to Amy. "Look Am, I don't want to make our anniversary a battle, but you're somewhere else, and I'm not sure what to do about it."

Amy feels bad for neglecting to focus on their date. She promises Mark that nothing is wrong with them. She assures him they are okay, but that something happened and she has been thinking about Kyle recently.

Mark responds in a calm but slightly annoyed tone, "Well what is it, what happened?"

Amy looks Mark up and down; hesitant to tell him about what has been distracting her. "Well… I was getting ready to shower today… an… and I got a message from Kyle's homework account…" She breaks down and wipes a tear away.

Mark takes a deep breath as he prepares to be straightforward with Amy.

"Kyle is gone, Am. He passed. I mean, someone is just messing with you. It isn't too hard to hack a homework app, it's 2017… Someone was bound to make a joke. This was the biggest news in town for years. I just feel it is getting a little bit too much and you are letting this get in the way of us."

Amy is flooded with shock. She can't believe how inconsiderate Mark is being. She jumps up from her chair. "Of course you're worried, Mark. When *aren't* you worried about yourself, or your own wellbeing, or not having an ass to press up against? Go to hell."

She storms out of the restaurant, almost knocking over the waiter who was on his way to serve their food.

Mark stands up, yelling, pleading for Amy to come back.

She exits and Mark sits back down, slams his fist on the table in fury, and opens up his phone.

Amy walks through town with no intention of going home.

She just wants to walk and walk until her mind focuses on something else. As she passes the church she receives a chat message from the online homework site. She gasps in fear, until she notices it is from Jamie. She is curious as to why Jamie did not just call or text her like usual.

She opens the message. It reads *did my last chat bother you?*

Amy stares at her phone in confusion. She types a message: *What do you mean Jamie? I haven't heard from it at all today girl ha-ha.*

Well maybe you should pay more attention.

43

Okay Jamie... What's going on? You seem really off.

The only thing that's off is going to be your man's head if you don't stop being such a dumb bitch.

At this point Amy realizes this is another prank and it is clearly not Jamie. She knows it must be the same person who is trying to scare her from Kyle's account. She doesn't answer this time. Another message arrives: *No response? Fine by me... Secret time is up. I know what you did. And soon, so will everyone else. You'll hear from me.*

Amy shoves her phone back in her purse. She has had enough of these sick pranks. She looks around to see the quiet, empty town that surrounds her, and she makes her way home for the night.

The following Monday after school, Amy has plans to meet Spencer for lunch. They haven't spoken since their dispute at the dance, and Amy feels more alone now than ever. Amy arrives at the corner coffee shop in town and takes a few spins around the café;

she cannot seem to find Spencer and assumes he is running late as usual. She proceeds to the counter to get a coffee.

While she waits, a hand grazes Amy's side and a voice from behind her says, "Make that two, on her tab."

Amy does not even need to turn around to know that it is Spencer. Rolling her eyes, she faces the lady at the cash register, gives a frustrated smile, and pays for both coffees.

The girl at the register wishes Amy luck with her 'boyfriend'. Amy assures the worker he is not, and never will be, her boyfriend. Then she chuckles while saying this and heads directly for a table.

Spencer raises his eyebrows and smiles obnoxiously at the worker as he follows Amy to the table. They sit, and he asks Amy why she has invited him here, and why she has been so insistent on meeting the past few days. Amy knows what Spencer's reaction is going to be when she tells him about the stalker's messages. She is prepared to be the laughing stock of Spencer's night. She begins to explain.

As she wraps up her past twenty-four hours, Spencer is not amused by what Amy has told him. He composes himself and shrugs his shoulders, interlocks his fingers and leans forward to Amy. "You need to stop obsessing over this already, Amy, I know you're sad, but this is getting to be too much. It's a harmless prank; no one is out to get you."

Amy tries to catch her breath from talking too fast. She asks Spencer how he can be so certain.

"Because if some magical person knows what happened that night, then they would be coming after me too... And guess what, no one is bothering me or accessing my homework account. So calm down and ignore it, otherwise you'll just fuel this person."

Amy stares at Spencer and realizes she may be overreacting to an extent, but insists he cannot blame her.

Spencer asks Amy if she thought it was at all curious that the first time this prank occurred was about ten minutes after she walked out on Mark at dinner.

Amy's face turns from calm and civil to insulted and outraged. She jumps up from the table, spilling her coffee mug onto the ground.

"Do not!" she yells. "There is no way Mark would attack me this way, he is a lot of things but he is not a monster..." She grabs her purse, drops a five-dollar bill for the waitress, and storms out of the café.

Two days after Amy and Spencer's attempt to rekindle their mutual tolerance of each other, they have to sit next to each other in study period. The door shoots open three minutes after the bell – Spencer is making a late appearance as usual. He weaves in and out of the rows to his seat in the back, directly to the right of Amy.

Amy stares down at her notebook and continues to write as if nothing around her has changed. Their teacher approaches the front of their row and starts passing out the study guides. Amy turns around to hand the rest to the girl behind her, then back towards the front of the room. Amy feels a ridge on the back of her study guide;

she flips it over to see a post-it note stuck to the back of the packet. *Rm. 158* is scribbled on the note in blue pen.

Amy turns towards Spencer but stops herself. He hasn't noticed, so she chooses to keep this secret. She raises her hand and requests to use the bathroom, so she can go look into Room 158, which is down the hall.

Amy's teacher grants her permission, and she quickly exits the room. Spencer notices Amy shooting out of her row, and looks up with curiosity. He watches until Amy is out of sight.

Amy makes a hard left at the end of the hall, in the opposite direction of the girl's bathroom. She walks as calmly and quickly as she can to the last door on the left, lunges to the doorknob and zips through the doorway. Her phone drops instantly as she lifts her hand to cover her mouth. She screams out in pure horror as she backs out of the closet.

There, in a broken chair, is the body of junior, Fred Dodson. He was not very well known, though he sat next to Amy in her French class. Fred has a golf-ball-sized bullet hole directly in the middle of his chest. He is pale and motionless; at a single glance it was clear he was gone.

Teachers tear out of their rooms like whack-a-mole machines in old arcades. They all see Amy on her knees in terror. Fred's body becomes unbalanced on the chair and falls out into the hallway.

Amy is in pure and utter shock. She is heaving and crying as she looks back and forth in terror. Spencer looks out into the hallway and makes direct eye contact with Amy. Scared and uncertain, he looks away. Everyone watching, even the teachers, are all motionless at what they have seen. The hallway is silent and all eyes are on Amy and on Fred's body...

Chapter III

An Alliance Formed

Shock does not begin to describe the look on Amy's face. She sits motionless in the guidance counselor's office as the school nurse cleans and disinfects Fred's blood from her arm. Anyone who knows Amy personally knows she could not be responsible for this. Others seem very skeptical and keep their distance from Amy. The nurse and principal ask Amy if she needs anything: water, change of clothes, her phone – but she sits without a word or a single movement. She has yet to utter a word since her piercing scream at the sight of Fred's body.

The teachers are beginning to seriously worry, and her parents have been summoned. Spencer comes in to see how she is doing. Shockingly, despite Spencer's usual inconsiderate behavior and lack of care for others, he felt he had to come see her. He tries to squeeze through the doorway which is blocked by the nurse and principal, but the nurse stops him and insists Amy is to have no visitors. Amy looks up when she hears Spencer's commotion at the door. She would like some comfort and a friendly face, but still cannot muster up the will to speak or ask for him. Spencer and Amy make eye contact and Spencer nods and smiles at her. Amy tries to smile but can barely lift the corners of her lips. The principal implores Spencer that it is time to go and that Amy's parents will be arriving shortly, along with the Gullburg police.

It is only 12:45pm and the school has closed early, for obvious reasons. The only remaining people in the building are Amy, the nurse, and the principal. The police arrive at the same moment as Amy's parents. Mr. and Mrs. Jameson race down the south hallway and enter the guidance counselor's office, to find Amy still sitting still as stone. Amy's father drops to his knees and hugs Amy as tight as he can, pulling away quickly to put his suit jacket around her shoulders.

"It's okay, honey. It's all going to be okay," Mr. Jameson whispers in Amy's ear as he continues patting her on the back.

He stands up, turns towards the nurse and principal, and hollers, "Now what in the hell happened? What kind of high school is being run here?"

One of the two cops in the room politely asks Mr. Jameson to calm down, insisting that his overreacting will not help anyone.

This does not sit well with Mr. Jameson, since his daughter just endured a frightening ordeal. He turns to the cops, frustrated, and asks if he has any kids of his own. The officer informs him that he does not.

Mr. Jameson chuckles and takes a step closer to the officer. "Then shut your damn mouth." He goes back to sit beside Amy.

The principal begs them to stop this verbal sparring, and wait for Sheriff Winston to arrive in a few minutes. The officer and Mr. Jameson look at each other, nodding to signify a mutual truce, knowing it is just their tempers talking.

Mrs. Jameson and the nurse remain in the far corner making small talk, avoiding all of the male confrontation. Amy and her mom make their first eye contact and share a warm smile, a smile that says, *we will get through this.* Sheriff Winston finally arrives and makes his way into the guidance office.

Handshakes are exchanged between the principal, Mr. and Mrs. Jameson, and the sheriff.

"I wish we were meeting under much better circumstances, folks," the sheriff says, "but this world today… there's always something."

The sheriff and Mr. Jameson know each other through work. Many crimes over the years have brought Sheriff Winston to the hospital that employs Amy's father. They also had been in contact recently due to Kyle's untimely death. Sheriff Winston finally heads over toward Amy and expresses his deepest sympathy for what she has just witnessed. As difficult as he expects it to be, he has no choice but to ask Amy if she has any information about this horrific act.

Mr. Jameson intervenes. "Of course she has no information. Why would she?"

Winston reiterates that he *has* to ask.

Amy interrupts them. "I do. I mean, I think I do…" She wipes the remaining tears from her face, smearing makeup across her face.

All eyes in the room turn to Amy. Mr. Jameson looks at Amy in confusion and concern.

Amy slowly opens her mouth and elaborates on her past few days. "Well, about four or five days ago I was messaged by Kyle's homework account. It really freaked me out at first, and it obviously upset me, but I assumed it was just a prank. It happened a second time after my anniversary dinner with Mark, and that was the last I heard from this person until today…"

Amy's father and the sheriff ask Amy what she means by "until today." She informs everyone about the post-it note stuck to her study guide, which directed her to the deceased body in Room 158. No one blames Amy for going to investigate the room alone. This was in her school, where she felt safe and secure. Unfortunately, that is not the case, and Amy feels she will not be safe anywhere for the foreseeable future.

Winston sits down next to Amy, rubbing her back and repositioning her father's jacket around her shoulders. "So you believe whoever was previously playing these games with you is the same person who is guilty of Fred's murder?"

Amy finally stops the tears and nods. The sheriff is flustered – as is everyone – by this new information. Winston instructs the principal to keep the school closed until he instructs him further. Mr. and Mrs. Jameson are not satisfied with the lack of action by Winston in response to this troubling news. They plead with the sheriff to take some type of action or precaution. He tells Mr. Jameson that he will start a trace on Amy's homework site for sent messages to any and all students. If nothing is discovered there, he will provide Amy with two 24-hour surveillance officers.

The sheriff puts his coat on and says goodbye to Amy. "Amy, one last thing... Do you have any clue why or what message this guy is trying to send? Why is he interested in the warehouse fire, and Kyle?"

Amy, who is not ready to admit that she and Spencer were somewhat at fault for Kyle's accident, shakes her head. "I have no idea, sir," she mumbles as Winston walks out of the office.

School resumes four days later, after a thorough search of the grounds, security camera inspection, and new guards on duty at all exits. However, Amy doesn't return when all the other students do. She is taking some extra time to herself at home for now. This is excused, and approved by her parents, so there is no trouble. Spencer is also taking some time off, although unauthorized, but this is Spencer's style.

The Monday everyone returns to school, Amy wakes up around 10 am. She rustles her blanket off her left shoulder and turns to her alarm clock which is still set to snooze, as it would be for a regular school day. She hits the button and makes her way out of her room.

Before she can leave she is startled by a sharp knock on her bedroom window. Jolting around to see what caused the noise, she sees Spencer hanging like Tarzan off a tree branch outside the window, waving and smiling. She walks towards the window and unlatches the lock so he can climb in. She goes to the lounge chair in her corner to sit down, crosses her legs, and waits to hear Spencer's reason for coming.

His backpack flies through the window, knocking Amy's lava lamp on the ground, followed by a very loud, "Umm, my bad..." Spencer then puts his leg through the window, climbs in, and shuts the window behind him. Amy asks Spencer very calmly what the hell he thinks he is doing.

He stands, picking up his backpack. "Morning to you too."

Amy isn't amused by Spencer's failure to answer her questions. Again, she asks why he is there.

Spencer makes himself at home on the foot of her bed and takes a deep breath, before the rant begins. "Look, what do you think? I thought you were freaking out, just being a girl and what not, but with Fred dying, and this supposed note you got... That means this could be real. If it's real, it's about Kyle, and I am just as guilty as you are, so I'm at your disposal. I'm all ears."

Amy has never been so caught off guard in her life, but she couldn't say she isn't extremely relieved.

Spencer still has a look of shock on his face. He can't believe someone could actually be holding their mistakes like an axe above their heads, and has taken a life in the process. "So what do we do, Amy?"

Amy feels uncertain about what to suggest, but she has been waiting forever for his cooperation. She is not going to waste it. "Well, I don't exactly have a plan, Spence. I haven't exactly gone through something like this before. It's not every day you are involved in your brother's death and someone comes after you for it, so I'm more than a bit distressed."

Spencer is shocked at the aggressive sarcasm, this being a side of Amy he has never seen before. He feels this whole situation really has her shaken up. He asks if she has any idea who could be doing this – who would want revenge for what happened to Kyle? Who would even know about it?

Amy shakes her head in confusion, at a loss for answers. She hasn't the slightest clue where to begin.

"Come on Amy. Anything? You're the only one this person has contacted. I can't ask anyone else."

Amy steps back and lightly falls onto the bed as if in disbelief. She is taken aback with a memory she had no idea she had, but feels it could be the answer to all the horror.

"What? What is it?" Spencer asks eagerly.

Amy explains that she may know who this person is, though she does not know a name or even a motive behind it. But, this is the best guess she has. She goes on to explain to Spencer about the odd, middle-aged woman with a limp that she saw observing Kyle's burial. That is all the description she can give, considering the woman was many yards away, almost as if she did not want anyone to know she was paying her respects.

Spencer's eyes light up with relief. He jumps up, almost hitting his head on the ceiling fan.

Amy busts a quick smirk followed by a sneaky chuckle at his reaction. This is the first Amy has felt anything but sad numbness in weeks.

Spencer shouts, "Oh my God, Amy! That's exactly what we need. Firstly, I can handle some injured soccer mom. Secondly, now if anything goes wrong we have a description and maybe some surveillance footage nearby the cemetery on the day of Kyle's service." He suggests that they wait for the next contact and try to meet with this individual, and leave the cops out of it.

Amy is uneasy with this plan and does not see the logic in it. Spencer assures her that if this person has hacked Kyle's account they can most likely see if they have contacted the cops. Amy knows that Spencer is right, but still does not like the idea.

Spencer explains to Amy that he will have two or three of his buddies from school follow close by, and they will handle the woman when she appears. Although Amy is still against the idea, she knows it may be the safest option. However, she also knows, deep down, that it could be the most dangerous plan as well. She knows they don't have the ball in their court, and they aren't able to be picky about which plan to execute.

She nods in agreement, gets up, walks towards Spencer and hugs him gently. "Thank you, really. This is my entire fault anyway."

Spencer pulls away and looks at Amy, and assures her that none of this would have happened without him. Regardless of who initiated the plan, they are both to blame.

The following week is quiet, with no more harassment or bloodshed. The town hopes this horrible rollercoaster ride is finally coming to an end. The Jamesons and the police do not feel this way. They know that no one puts on a show like that inside a school full of students just once, with no explanation. They have no new information, and they are still unsure about why this person cares so much about Kyle's death. That is the only thing Amy and Spencer

61

knew that everyone else do not. The two of them are weighing the idea of telling the cops and her parents the truth behind it all, but they just can't. The guilt is too much, and they can't ruin their lives just before college. They would both be viewed as accessories and charged with involuntary manslaughter, so for now they continue to handle this on their own.

A few days later, Amy returns to school. She feels it is time to try to get back into her regular routine. Everyone has their eyes locked on Amy from the second she enters school that day. This is the longest and most uncomfortable walk of her life. She feels as if she has concrete shoes, and cannot walk fast enough to avoid the looks.

The walk from the entrance to her classroom is maybe forty yards away, but to Amy it feels like the length of two football fields. She finally reaches the end of her very unpleasant gauntlet and closes her homeroom door behind her. The halls seem to echo her return. To all these uninformed students, Amy is just a regular girl whose brother has recently passed away, and who then found a dead body at school. That is the extent of their knowledge, so no one could really blame them for being a bit frightened or distant towards her.

Amy sits down in her homeroom. Now she has a whole new room of people ready to focus their attention on her. It is slightly less painful than her walk down the hallway but, nonetheless, all eyes are still set on her.

There is no class professor since this is a study period, so most students are catching up on work they should have completed last night. Amy's seat happens to be toward the back, where she and Mark used to sit. Mark switched study halls immediately after their breakup, so only Amy is now in the back. Amy looked at Mark's seat and stares out into space for a minute or so. She hasn't heard from or seen Mark since their fight at dinner. The thought of Mark being the person responsible for doing this to her has crossed her mind. She cannot help but wonder or be curious. She does not want to think he is capable of doing such things, and she never thought he would hurt her like this, regardless of their status.

She returns to reality after her horrid daydream. She snaps out of the thought that Mark is doing this. "It just could not be him, it's the lady, I know it…" Amy mumbles to herself, taking deep breaths.

The student sitting in front of Amy turns around quickly, asking what she said. Amy apologizes and claims she was just talking to herself. This was not a good look for the girl everyone already thought might be going a bit crazy. Amy goes back to attempting to study and tries to focus. A loud, high-pitched bell sounds, its old age evident in its rattling ring. An announcement begins: "Amy Jameson, please report to the call office. Amy, please report to the call office."

All eyes in the class are on Amy once again. Everyone is curious as to what could be going on. Amy, who is just as concerned and intrigued as her classmates, stands and makes her way towards the office.

She arrives at the first-floor office and takes a seat in the waiting area, awaiting further information about her summons. She expects to be visiting with the principal, as she assumes this has to have something to do with the investigation. However, it is not the principal who wants to see her: the principal's secretary asks Amy to come get a message that has been left for her.

The secretary tells Amy that the funeral parlor called and informed them they have found Amy's necklace, which was left in their bathroom at the viewing. The secretary tells Amy that she can pick it up anytime today after 3:30pm. Amy asks why the funeral parlor did not just call her house or her, but the secretary has no further information and has no further interest in the matter.

"They said they couldn't reach your parents. Next!" the secretary calls out, waving Amy away and gesturing the next person in line to come forward.

Amy rolls her eyes at the overweight, loud, nasty and even smelly secretary, and leaves the office. She stops at the bathroom on the way back to study hall, takes her phone out of her pocket, and sends Spencer a text: *Heading to funeral home after school to get the necklace I forgot. Can you drive me?*

Spencer responds quickly since he's also in study hall: *Of course*. Amy leaves the bathroom and goes on with her day, enjoying no contact from their stalker.

The day comes to an end and Amy is alone, waiting by Spencer's truck. He comes running out the gym door, tripping over his gym clothes still stuck around his ankles – he was in a rush to skip his open gym. Amy hangs her head to the side, still waiting for Spencer to crawl his way to the truck.

"Always so quick and smooth," Amy says with a laugh.

In a hurry, Spencer gets in the other side of the truck. "Do you want to go or not?" He pulls out of the south gym parking lot, peeling out hard to the right. The tires of the truck let out a screech so loud that his coach hears it from inside the gym.

They are about ten minutes away from the funeral home, in stock-still lunchtime traffic at the town square. Spencer musters up the strength to ask Amy a question he has been pondering for some time. He takes a deep breath and asks her if she thinks that Mark had any hand in what has been going on. Ironically, this has been in the back of Amy's mind too, since she was just considering it herself earlier today. She doesn't want Spencer to even know she has had the thought. She shuts his idea down immediately, assuring him that Mark would never takes things this far. Spencer feels a bit guilty for even asking and putting the thought in her head. He nods; accepting and respecting her answer, and continues driving.

They pull up to the funeral home and park in the guest lot at the side. They both slam their doors and head through the entrance. A cold, silent, and deserted vibe overcomes them upon their entrance. No one is in sight, and there is no desk attendant. Amy rings the small bell that sits on the desk beside the sign-in sheet. It echoes eerily throughout the funeral parlor, but still no one comes.

Spencer grows agitated and impatient. "They go through all this trouble to call school, and now they're too busy? The hell is that?"

Amy is not pleased either, but she does not have as short a temper as Spencer. She asks Spencer to quite down and wait a minute. He does not approve that suggestion, as he throws the desk door open and walks in the back searching for employees. Amy tells him to come back and stop. He does not pay Amy's comment any mind.

Spencer continues past the office and trash room and still has yet to see anyone. He stares down the long hallway.

Amy yells again for him to come back, but he does not respond. This aggravates Amy and she pushes past the door to go after him. She looks down past the offices and doesn't see any sign of him yet. "Spence? C'mon, Spence!" she calls out. There is still no answer as she moves closer to the trash room.

As she turns the corner she is thrown back by a hooded figure, moving past her so swiftly that she falls. She looks up to see a swinging door but no one in sight. She has no earthly idea what the figure looked like beneath his hood. His face had looked rather grey, but she could not tell if it was a beard or a mask of some sort.

She gets to her feet, rubbing her right elbow which was bruised when she tripped and fell. She sees Spencer's leg behind the furthest trash bin. She knows it's happening again.

Her pulse skips a beat and her breath shortens. She closes her eyes, barely peeking as she approaches the corner. She hesitates, praying what she thinks is happening is not true.

She looks over the top of the cart. She gasps in relief to see that Spencer is badly injured but still alive. His arm has a deep hole that looks as though it was made by a small pick axe. Blood is flowing from the wound onto the floor and Amy's boot is nearly covered in it. It continues to flow. She gets to her knees and slaps Spencer's face repeatedly, attempting to keep him conscious.

He has already passed out and is unresponsive. Amy, who is now, unfortunately, getting used to handling these situations, frantically reaches for Spencer's phone to call the cops. She dials incorrectly, hearing only a dial tone. She rubs Spencer's chest again hoping he will respond. Finally, the 911 operator picks up.

"Hi. Hello. My friend's hurt. He's stabbed! He's bleeding! Please! Help us! We're at... Umm, I don't know the address. It's the funeral parlor, the Letterman Funeral Home."

"Okay, okay, I'm sending a car. Just stay calm and take deep breaths, miss. Stay calm." The operator continues to soothe Amy and asks her questions. Is she safe? Does she have a description of the attacker? She is doing her best to keep Amy busy and to keep her mind off the horror before her.

Amy asks if the operator will remain on the line until the officers arrive, and the operator is pleased to do so. Spencer is still unconscious, and they are still alone in the funeral home.

She hears a movement from the far door in the room. She is stiff as a board, full of nerves, not knowing who is approaching. She is relieved to see it is just one of the sheriff's junior deputies, followed by backup.

The deputies file quickly into the room and help Amy to her feet and out of the room, so they can tend to Spencer. A gurney is rolled in and Spencer is lifted onto it quickly and safely. Amy sits on a stool as one of the EMT assistants tends to her.

They push Spencer's gurney past her quickly and to the exit where the ambulance is located. Connor and Jamie run through the door as Spencer is wheeled out. One of the deputies directs them to Amy to comfort her. The EMT finishes up: Amy has only suffered a minor bruise and a scratched elbow.

Connor and Jamie instantly bombard her with questions: "Who did it?" "What's going on?" "Is he okay?" "What were you guys doing?"

Amy is flustered by all the talk. She belts out, "Guys, Guys, listen. Stop, give me a minute. I don't know if he is alright... I'll explain the rest on the way over to the hospital."

They both put their arms around Amy and walk her toward the car.

Chapter IV

Family Secrets

The police car escorting Amy pulls into the ER entrance. Amy jumps out of the car before it even comes to a stop. Connor and Jamie are already waiting at the door. They all start to run to Spencer's room. They arrive but are not allowed in – the tending nurse informs them that Spencer is in the process of getting stitches and that they will have to wait until he is conscious again. The three friends find a spot in the waiting area and set up camp for the next few hours in the hospital. They have no intentions of going anywhere until they see that Spencer is alright.

They all sit in silence, Connor and Jamie still with their eyes locked on Amy. "So everything you just told us, everything that has happened... it's all about someone being mad at you guys for drugging Kyle?" Connor asks.

Amy looks up at them, struggling to look either of them in the eye due to her self-loathing. "Not only drugged. We basically killed him, guys..." she says.

She makes them promise not to say anything at all until she says so. Connor and Jamie are on board; they would do anything to help Amy and Spencer. They are extremely taken back and shocked at the news, but they put that aside in order to get to the bottom of everything, without informing the police of Amy's actions. Connor offers to go get some coffee for everyone and heads off to search for the cafeteria. Amy looks to Jamie and asks if she should call Spencer's parents or something. She is still all out of sorts and feels horribly responsible for what has happened to him. Jamie assures Amy that the medics will have already have done that. She envelops Amy in a generous hug.

The visitor entrance doors shoot open, startling Amy and Jamie.

"Zach!" Jamie shouts, and runs into his arms.

Amy, still stuck with so many questions, waits for their hello to end so Jamie can explain.

"Amy – you remember Zach? He was the DJ from our last dance?"

Amy nods, but can't hide her confusion. Jamie explains that they have been seeing each other since the day after the dance, when he kindly turned those jocks in the right direction.

"Well, nice to see you again Zach," Amy says. "I never actually met you, but nice to see you. Thanks for coming."

He promises her that it's no trouble at all, and that he is happy to be there. Connor walks back in, juggling three hot coffees, though a stain on his shirt shows that the attempt has not been totally successful. Sheriff Winston and a pack of deputies follow quickly on his heels. As the sheriff approaches Amy, he asks what has happened. Amy explains how she and Spencer were asked to stop by the funeral home to pick up the necklace she had left behind at Kyle's wake, and that she got the message from school and never talked to the funeral home people directly.

The sheriff asks her why they didn't just call her parents, and why they called the school. Amy has no answer, and continues to avoid the truth about the night of the fire.

"Okay... keep calm. It's alright," Sheriff Winston says as he puts his arm around Amy's shoulder. He asks her to just simply explain the attack, including any details she can think of.

Amy starts to tremble. "We just came here after school as instructed. I rang the bell and no one came. Spencer got hotheaded like he always does, and went back to look for someone. He didn't respond to me, so I went back to look, and someone pushed me over and ran out the door. They were wearing a hood, with some type of grey face guard. I don't know what it was." She takes a deep breath.

The sheriff ponders the detail of this grey face guard; he wants to know more about that. Sadly, Amy truly has no other information. He walks Amy back over to the nurse and her friends. Before they reach the others, Amy grabs the sheriff's shirt and pulls him aside to tell him about the lady she saw at Kyle's funeral. She tells him how she saw the lady in the distance at Kyle's service. She describes the lady – hooded, with a limp, but not too old.

The sheriff asks Amy why she thinks this lady might be involved. Amy feels confident that there was something off about her. Not having much more to go on, the sheriff has no choice but to take Amy's word and attempt to investigate this woman.

The only other person who encountered this mystery lady was, unfortunately, Kyle – and, clearly, he cannot be asked. Not a soul had any idea that Kyle saw her the night he died. The question now is: who is this woman? What is her interest in Kyle? What could have sparked these vengeful actions?

With nothing to go on but a brief description, the sheriff leaves to put word out for the mystery woman.

Amy inches back towards the three kids and the nurse. The nurse lets them know that their visit to Spencer must be very brief, but he can be seen quickly.

"Oh. Okay. My God, of course," Jamie says.

Amy tells them to go ahead; she is going to wait at the door for her parents to arrive. They all nod and give comforting smiles, then follow the nurse down the hall. Amy receives a new message from her secret friend, sent from Kyle's same school login.

You told sheriff too much. This was a matter between you and me. No need for outsiders, there will be consequences.

Before Amy can even think about responding, he signs off. Amy is beyond torn at this point. This person was angered by her telling the police about the woman. She realized how quickly her tormentor found this out. He truly had to have eyes and ears everywhere. Amy was starting to lose faith, she wondered if everyone could certainly be trusted. This leads Amy to think how bothered the killer would feel if she ever got the courage to tell the police about her role in Kyle's accident. She now fully realizes this is not something that can be solved with arrests and handcuffs. But more importantly, why they would kill to avenge him? Seconds later, Amy's mom and dad walk in the door and envelop her in a group hug which lasts for several seconds.

"Are you alright, sweetie?" Amy's mom says.

Amy musters a small smile and assures her that she will be okay.

Her dad is furious, and is already demanding answers about what is going on. "How did this person get to you guys? What happened, Amy?" he says, loud enough for everyone in the room to hear.

Amy begs her dad to lower his voice and take a deep breath. She does not feel like having the entire hospital hearing this conversation.

Mr. Jameson realizes she is right and apologizes to Amy for his temper, expressing that he is just so worried about her and everything going on.

Amy leads her parents down the hall to join everyone in Spencer's room. They pass the doorway and see Spencer in his bed. His eyes are open, and he is a bit pale. He is receiving some extra oxygen and having his heart monitored as a safety precaution. He takes off the oxygen mask to greet Amy and her parents. Amy can't help but let out a massive smile, shed a tear, and lunge at Spencer. She hugs him as tightly as possible, as he lies motionless in his hospital bed. Connor and Jamie greet Mr. and Mrs. Jameson, and they reciprocate this greeting.

"I wish it was under better circumstances, but it is great to see you two," Mrs. Jameson says. "How are you holding up? Are you two doing alright?"

Jamie and Amy's mother share a hug. Connor and Zach stand nearby, talking quietly.

Jamie pulls away. "Yeah, thanks Mrs. J. I just can't get used to this. It's like a shock that never goes away, it just lingers. Oh, I am so rude! Mr. and Mrs. Jameson, this is my boyfriend Zach. We actually met at the last school dance that we all went to. Some drunken football player I didn't know was bothering me all night and this gem handled that, and then swept me away."

Mrs. Jameson reaches out to shake Zach's hand. "Well it is great to meet you as well, Zach. Like I said, I wish it was under any other circumstance, but it was very nice of you to join Jamie here today."

Zach is honored, and feels so much comfort and acceptance from everyone in the room.

However, Amy's dad, who is a bit aggravated as usual, does not seem to be as welcoming as everyone else. He does not know Zach, and is on edge about anything out of the ordinary. Mr. Jameson gives Zach a very unpleasant look as he asks the entire room if it seems odd this DJ has just decided to stick around.

Amy's jaw drops. She is infuriated about how rude her dad is being. Jamie now feels a bit out of place and awkward, and keeps to herself as Zach puts his arm around her.

Amy gets in her dad's face and expresses her frustration. "Dad, he is here because he likes Jamie, who is one of our best friends. It is very nice of him. I know you are scared, but do you think I'm not? Hold it in check for me, please."

Everyone in the room turns their attention back to what truly matters: Spencer. He slowly starts sitting up, grunting and staying off the rib wound on his right side. Amy pushes past her parents and hugs Spencer very gently, trying to avoid his sore area.

"So it only took a small pick axe in my side for you to show me some love, huh?" Spencer jokes.

Amy laughs and wipes a tear from her face. Never has she been so relieved. She was dreading the possibility of being responsible for the loss of his life. She was dying for this all to end, but it has brought her and Spencer together. She feels that it will be a tremendous help in getting through these struggles. She has started to appreciate him more and more.

Everyone rushes Spencer with love, affection, and relief that he had survived.

"I guess I'll introduce myself to this Zach fellow first, seeing as how no one has been polite enough to welcome him yet," Spencer says, glancing at Mr. Jameson.

Amy, along with almost everyone in the room, grins at his comment. It warms them to see he did not lose his sense of humor or his light mood.

Spencer grunts as he finally situates himself in an upright position. Amy finally has to ask if he saw the face of who did this. Everyone peers in, desperately awaiting an answer.

Spencer is not thrilled to inform them that this person came at him from behind. "He grabbed me from behind and just got me right in my side. I fell and then he ran out. I only saw his boots, and a hooded sweatshirt from behind."

Amy blurts out that that must have been when she heard the commotion and turned the corner to meet the stranger.

"Great, so we have nothing," Jamie says. "This is not good."

The sheriff strides in. "Amy, we're going to have to set you up with protective detail. If this lady with a limp is following you, that'll be our best chance to grab her. So any contact from our guy on that chat site, you tell us this time… No more super hero solo missions, got it?"

Amy acquiesces to these demands and nods her head. Mr. and Mrs. Jameson ask what he means about a lady. Amy has not told her parents this detail yet, she has just informed everyone today. Spencer was the only one who already knew.

"There was a middle-aged woman with a limp at Kyle's burial," Amy says. "I didn't think anything of it at the time, but I think she may be the one doing this. I just don't know why."

Mrs. Jameson calls out to her husband, "A limp? Honey, doesn't your secretary, Jenny, have a limp?"

"Yeah, Jenny does," Mr. Jameson replies. "From when she fell off that ladder, while doing the files last fall."

Amy's mom has a look of relief on her face. She suggests that Jenny probably came to the funeral just to pay her respects as her dad's employee. Mr. Jameson agrees, and assures Amy that it was most likely just Jenny. They do not want Amy to send the police on unnecessary chases and divert their focus.

Amy pleads with the sheriff and her parents to trust her, and let her and the police attempt to trap her. "I just have a feeling about her," she says quietly.

"Alright. I will send someone to confirm if this was your father's secretary, if that's the case," the sheriff says. "We will have to assume she was just paying respects at the funeral, Amy." He wishes them a safe day and exits the room.

Moments after, the nurse tending to Spencer comes in to change his IV. "Hey, guys. Oh, hey there, Mr. Jameson. I haven't seen you lately. I hate to do this, but I am going to have to kick you all out for a few moments. I'll make it as quick as possible."

They all cooperate and file out of the room.

"How did you know the nurse, Dad?" Amy asks.

"Oh I do a lot of medical consulting with this branch," he replies. "I meet with a new nurse every month."

Amy and her parents head back out towards the entrance, followed by Connor, Jamie, and Zach.

"I'm going to get a ride back to our house with Connor and them, alright, guys?" Amy says to her parents.

They both wrap an arm around Amy and hug her, both kissing her on the head.

"We'll see you soon." Mrs. Jameson says as she walks out the door, waving at everyone.

Amy turns back to the group; "Well, now that we are done with the questions from the sheriff and my parents, we can talk a bit."

Jamie tells her they are here for her, and ready to listen.

Connor takes the floor. "So, from what you have told us after you and Spence knocked Kyle out and, well, you know... Someone knows about it, and thinks you both should pay."

Amy informs them that they now know just as much as she does, and she has a lack of answers. Zach asks how anyone would even know that, and who would take it this far. They are all at a loss for suggestions.

"That is what we need to find out," Amy says. "We need to start with who cared for Kyle this much, and who would be this angered by what happened."

She lets the three of them head out to bring the car around, and she goes to say goodbye and goodnight to Spencer. She tells him she will be back as soon as she can with answers. Spencer, being a man of action usually, is having difficulty watching this unravel from the vantage point of a hospital bed. He thanks Amy, and she shuts the door behind her.

Connor pulls up to Amy's house and parks the car. Connor and Zach continue to Jamie's house, next door. Zach does his best to cheer Amy up. He lets them know he has a small amount of knowledge about computer coding, and would look into the chats when they get sent to her. Amy thanks them all so much for their support, and for not judging her about the night of the fire. She is really moved by their trust and friendship.

She goes into her house to spend time with her parents, but as soon as she goes through her front door she walks into a lion's-den dispute between her mother and father. Amy is flustered. She expected to come into a quiet house and spend some time with them after this long horrid day. That was apparently not on the agenda for the Jameson's this evening.

"That's a lie and you know it!" Mrs. Jameson shouts as she squeezes past Amy. She slams the bathroom door behind her.

Amy's father looks down at the kitchen island he is leaning on and sighs. He rubs his eyes, hoping to massage the stress away.

Amy stands there as still as stone, with her eyes locked on her father and awaits an explanation. "Dad, what isn't true? What's wrong with Mom?"

Mr. Jameson stands up straight and takes his hand off the counter. He puts his hands on Amy's arms. She looks back at him with confusion, and a bit of fear. "Your mother is just overreacting. I had two business dinners that included the nurse from today and my secretary. Your mother is all sad and upset with this she is putting ideas in her mind that aren't factual."

Amy trembles and moves a few steps back from her father, "Wait. Dad, you weren't with these two women...?" she mutters in a fearful tone.

Amy's dad cannot look her in the eye. He looks down, assuring Amy that he isn't lying to her. "There were no feelings, these were business trips gone wrong. I love your mom, Amy!"

Amy is already half way out of the kitchen, in tears, heading toward her room. "Am... Amy!" her dad yells again, to no response. He chugs the remains of his whiskey rocks, and throws the glass at the fridge. The glass shatters and picture magnets of relatives and his children fall to the floor. Too full of rage and frustration, he leaves the mess and goes out the front door for a drive to a motel, since no one in the house wants to see or speak to him.

Amy is too broken to leave her room and see her mother. She is sure that her mom wants some time alone. Amy hears her dad's car start, and the headlights shine into her bedroom window as he pulls out of the driveway.

She looks out as the car heads to the right down the road. She starts to wonder if maybe her dad had something to do with all of this. She does not know how or why, and she knows he would never hurt Kyle or Amy. Amy now has a whole new set of facts and thoughts to work through if she wants all of this to come to an end. It is only becoming more complicated, and she has fewer people she can trust.

She wants to take care of this on her own, as fast as she can. The boy-crazy party girl she once knew is gone, and she has a whole new outlook on her life and herself. She now knows this will all shape her into the person she will be for the rest of her life. She knows who she once was, and who she wanted to be.

Chapter V

Secrets Revealed

A couple weeks pass. Amy's father comes in and out of the house briefly. He grabs work files, attempts to converse with Amy, but normally she ignores him during each visit.

Amy has not heard her mother speak on this topic. Her mom has been hesitant to voice her views to Amy. Amy and her mom feel like they are all each of them has left at this point. Ever since the fire, they cannot help but notice that their family is deteriorating. They wonder if that is exactly what this stalker wants. More importantly, they start to think this is all connected. But they are missing a critical piece of the puzzle.

Amy knows this is the worst time to consider telling her mom the truth about what she and Spencer did to Kyle. Amy has barely gotten used to being responsible for all of this... She couldn't bear putting this burden on her mother, especially after her father's adulterous secrets have come to the surface.

Amy's mother walks into the kitchen while Amy is preparing her breakfast.

"Sheriff Winston called this morning, Am. He said he did speak to Jenny, your father's whore of a secretary, and she did pay her respects at the funeral. But she claims she has an alibi for Spencer's attack. He says for now he can keep an eye out, but he cannot charge her for as much as running a red light at this point."

Amy is not pleased with the response or the effort that the sheriff seems to be putting into his investigations. Amy already has a gut feeling about Jenny, but now she believes Jenny has a motive. Since finding out about her father's affair, she is not looking into new suspects. Amy tells her mom that she does not agree with Winston, and does not think he understands.

Amy suggests that they tell the sheriff about her father's actions; she feels it may be important information.

Her mom instantly shoots down her request. "Our business is our business. We already have the entire town curious about what happened to Kyle, and why this is happening now. We do not need any more exposure. We keep that to ourselves."

Amy does not want to argue. For once she totally agrees with her mother. She promises she will not say anything.

A breeze comes through the kitchen, followed by a sound of creaking metal, like an old porch swing slowing down. They both look toward the front door to see the mail slot cover waving back and forth.

A piece of mail rests on the ground. This strikes Amy as odd – there should be no post on Sunday. She pushes her coffee aside and walks to grab the mail.

As she bends down to grab it, her mom asks, "What is it, Am?"

"I'm not sure," Amy says in confusion. "It's addressed to both of us."

She tears apart the envelope as quickly as she can, but carefully so she does not damage what is inside. It contains a piece of paper folded three times, like a formal letter. When she unfolds it she notices the paper is sturdy and rough, almost like photo paper.

Once fully unfolded, she sees that on the other side of the paper is an X-ray image of someone's skull. Amy has no clue what to make of this, nor does she even know whose X-ray this is or why she's received it. She walks over to her mom to show her. Sadly, her mom is just as lost as she is and very scared.

"Who could this be Amy? Why? What is going on?" Mrs. Jameson says, as she hugs Amy.

Amy keeps staring at this picture over her mom's shoulders while they continue to hug. She is startled when she turns the paper over to set it down. She sees writing on the back of the sheet. She pulls away from her mom with a quick jolt and points to it.

The message reads: *No chance you'll ever see me coming.*

Amy and her mom look at each other, worried, confused, and at a loss. Who is this person? Why would they send an X-ray of themselves to Amy? They cannot wrap their head around all the incidents and taunting clues.

"We have to take this straight to Sheriff Winston, Am. This is a new ball game. We cannot play around with this anymore."

Amy agrees and knows that is the next move for them. They leave the house in a rush, the coffee pot still on and the laundry still running.

They pull out of their driveway and head towards the police station. Amy still holds the piece of mysterious mail, while turning the steering wheel. A few blocks from the station Amy notices a silver Toyota which seems to be following them. She does not say anything to her mom; she does not want her to worry or interfere. She decides to attempt to try to evade the trailing car, while keeping her mom out of the loop. She pulls into the next gas station, acting as if she needs to use the restroom.

"We're just a few blocks away, can't you wait?" Mrs. Jameson yells to Amy out the car window, as she makes her way towards the gas station.

Amy walks to the cashier and asks to use the key for the outdoor restroom. She has no intention of actually using the bathroom. She peers out the window to see that the silver Toyota has pulled in, and has stopped at a gas pump.

She can't make out who is in the driver seat, but to be safe, she continues to handle this situation surreptitiously. She walks down the right side of the gas station toward the bathroom door, passes the door and makes a lap around to the other side of the gas station. This brings her to the far side of the lot; the Toyota is located right around the corner. Amy peeks around the building and rubs up against the bricks. She wants to be as discreet as possible. She is determined to find out who's following her.

She slowly walks up to the car, out of view of all mirrors. This person has made it very clear they are not joking; they have taken lives and plan to take more. Amy is so lost and flustered, she is not thinking straight. She is about to confront this maniac on her own, with no defense.

She takes her final step toward the vehicle and opens the door, dragging the woman onto the ground, as she is not strong enough to pull her upright. Amy then pulls the woman onto her feet, but she falls back down to the ground. She stumbles, trying to get up while Amy stands over her. Amy notices how difficult it is for her to get up from her knees. She seems to have the same limp Amy has seen before.

"Jenny…?"

The woman who Amy now suspects to be her father's secretary and mistress and Amy's stalker now gets to her feet.

She meets Amy at eye level. "I swear I can explain everything."

Amy has never felt such rage in her entire life. She rocks back and slams her fist into Jenny's nose. Jenny falls back to the ground as Amy towers over her.

"You can explain a shit ton to Sheriff Winston, right now. Get in the back of our car."

Amy's mom pulls the car up and sees what has happened. She recognizes Jenny and sees her bloody nose. She is confused and at a loss, but she is not outraged by this scenario. Clearly, she is feeling animosity toward her husband's secretary.

Amy walks to her mom's window as she rolls it down. "We are taking her to the station. If she's only guilty of being a slut, let's let her prove it."

Mrs. Jameson has never been so shocked in her life. Amy has never so much as broken a nail before, and she has never seen in her determined. Jenny rises to her feet, and Amy blocks her exit.

"Okay, okay. I'll come with you to see the sheriff. I apologize but I didn't know you could go to jail for being part of an affair." Jenny says. She pushes past Amy and gets into the back seat of their car. Amy gets in and they pull away.

Amy asks Jenny why she has been following her, and suggests that she tell them before they get to the station.

"I think there's a wrench at your feet Am, if she gets all annoying," Mrs. Jameson says,

97

Amy cuts her off instantly. "Mom, stop. Jesus." She looks back to Jenny and awaits an answer, "So? Why are you doing all of this?"

Jenny holds her hands up and takes a deep breath, looking as if she is about to tell the longest story ever told. She blurts out at a rapid speed, "Okay, first off, I'm so sorry. Hate me. I would hate me, but I'm sorry. Do with it what you will, ladies." She looks at Amy's mom. "I'm sure you know I wasn't the only side dish your husband had..."

Mrs. Jameson and Amy share a look of deep sadness as Jenny continues, "So I went a bit off the deep end. I really started to like your dad and I heard so much about you and Kyle. I wanted to know more about you guys, I kind of cared about you. I realized it when I was so hurt by your dad telling me I was just a number. If I startled, or bothered you, it was never my intention. Then, after Kyle's accident, I just wanted to be there for you. You seemed so torn apart. I know I should respect your boundaries. You won't see me again, I promise. I need to move on."

Amy asks her if that is all she has done. She asks if Jenny had anything to do with the murder, or Spencer's attack.

Jenny looks dazed and genuinely confused. "What? No. Of course not. I read about the student death in school, but I don't know anything about an attack on your friend Spencer. I don't recall it in the news. Why would that be relevant to me watching out for you?"

Amy now has no idea who this stalker could be. She wants a culprit, but despite Jenny's horrible actions she seems genuine. She seems a bit crazy, but honest – and not harmful or evil.

"Okay, I think I believe you," Amy says, "and we will both let you go, as soon as you tell this to the police, and help us narrow down who's doing these things. You owe us that much."

Jenny agrees and sits back comfortably, touched that Amy is taking her at her word. They pull into the station and walk into the lobby, Amy and her mother side by side ahead of Jenny. They reach the front desk, and Mrs. Jameson tells them they must see the sheriff immediately.

The receptionist informs them that he is finishing up a press conference, but they can see him shortly. Since Jenny has nowhere to be, they did not see any harm in waiting. This gives Amy and her mom some time to ask Jenny some more questions.

"If you have been watching over me, have you seen anyone else odd or creepy around me?" Amy asks.

Jenny lets them know that she has never seen anything like that. "I only watched you and Kyle from time to time. I never had kids of my own and I started to think of you as my own."

Amy and her mom look at each other and then back at Jenny and both blurt out, "And Kyle?"

Jenny does not see why that is such a huge issue, but she explains how she anonymously bought Kyle a drink when he snuck into a bar one night.

Amy asks her which night this was. After careful consideration, Jenny concludes it was the night of Kyle's accident, but several hours earlier. Amy and her mom are desperate and demand that she think hard about anything she could have noticed

that night, or a person Kyle could have been with.

"Whoever is doing this feels very close to Kyle and is a mess

due to his death," Amy says frantically. "He did not talk to many

people. Anyone you saw may help."

Jenny thinks again but has nothing for them. She tells them

that Kyle was alone that night, and any other time she saw him.

Amy puts her hands on her face and stares down at the floor.

Her mom rubs her back and comforts her. "It'll be okay

Amy. Process of elimination – we'll find something out."

Amy feels a little better, but not safer since they have no new

leads. The sheriff finally walks through the double door amidst

flashes and questions, the aftermath of the press conference.

"This is one I can't hold off much longer people!" he yells.

"Let's find who's doing this and get our town back to normal, for

fuck sake. Get to work!" The sheriff rarely speaks or even raises his

voice, so his command gets every deputy locked onto their work.

Winston sees Amy and her mom in the waiting area across the room. As he walks over he notices the lady with them. "Who's this, ladies? What's going on?"

"Well a lot has happened that you aren't aware of yet," Amy says.

She is interrupted by her mother. "Amy, private..."

"Nothing is private and we are out of options," Amy responds. "He needs to know everything."

Mrs. Jameson does not want to be the laughing stock of the town and be further embarrassed, but she knows she needs to focus on the big picture: protecting Amy and the town.

Amy rattles off to the sheriff all about all that they have learned. She covers it all: her parents' fight, the affairs, her dad moving out, and how Jenny swears she was just looking out for them.

The sheriff's head is spinning as he attempts to retain this information. "So let me get this straight, girls. This is the secretary your father was having an affair with, her limp is due to an office accident, and then she followed his kids around because she is extra affectionate? Sounds like weeks of wasted of time to me." He sighs and rubs his hands over his face. "And you are certain she isn't involved? I would prefer to talk to this Jenny myself."

Amy and her mom completely agree. They tell the sheriff she has already agreed to give a full statement. The sheriff looks between Amy and her mom and then at Jenny. He beckons for her to follow him. Jenny follows Sheriff Winston to the interrogation room, as Amy and her mom go into the next room to get coffee.

Roughly thirty minutes pass, and the sheriff returns, followed by Jenny. The sheriff approaches Amy and her mom. He is holding a folder, which he slaps gently into Amy's chest, handing it to her.

"This is the statement she gave us," the sheriff says in exhaustion. "If it matches the story as told to you, we have no choice but to drop any suspicion of her."

He also informs them that she has an alibi for the attacks. Amy and her mom are not surprised by this – they believe Jenny,

103

they just don't like her. Amy and her mom skim through the file, and it seems to match Jenny's previous claim word for word. At this point Jenny is guilty only of home-wrecking, though maybe she needs a psychiatrist.

The sheriff tells them that he is going to have a deputy take Jenny back to her car. "Yeah, I heard you two didn't really give Jenny a choice in coming here today," he says in a disciplined tone, but with a bit of a smirk on his face.

Amy and her mom avoid eye contact with the sheriff. He tells them to hang in there; it has been a few weeks since Spencer's attack and there has been no contact.

Amy interrupts him. "Umm, actually that's not exactly true. We were actually already on our way in here today to talk to you about something, and then we happened to run into Jenny..."

Sheriff Winston looks curious and asks what they want to discuss.

Amy reaches into her pocket and hands the sheriff the photo paper and the envelope. He studies the paper and the message on the back. He is overwhelmed with how far and deep this person is getting into this. "Jesus H. Christ... We'll check it for prints, and look into all postal services for now. Do you know why this is the picture they sent? Or who it is?"

Amy has no idea, nor does she have any experience identifying people via their X-rays. She feels useless and powerless. She has gained nothing that might get her any closer to finding this person, and her family is falling apart.

Amy and her mom don't have any particular interest in saying any goodbyes to Jenny. The deputy walks her out, and takes her back to the gas station.

Before they leave, the sheriff implores the Jameson girls to hang in there, and also expresses his concern about their father not living at home. "Considering we do not know exactly what this person wants, despite the uncomfortable situation, don't you both think it's safest to all remain together?"

Amy and her mother look at each other and share a quick telepathic conversation: "I love him," Amy says. "He's my dad, but what he did will not change. I would prefer to not be angry at him throughout this ordeal, and seeing him will only cause me to be angry."

Her mom nods in agreement and they head out the front door of the station. The sheriff asks no further questions and dismisses them, he does not want to pry or intrude on their privacy. Amy and her mom leave the station, and the sheriff goes back to trying to find some answers for them.

An hour or so passes, and Amy and her mom stop for a bite to eat. With everything going on, and the recent discoveries, they just want a few hours to themselves. They arrive home from the diner around 9:15pm. Mrs. Jameson says she needs a hot shower, and cup of tea. Amy insists that her mom goes upstairs and starts the water, and she will handle the tea. Mrs. Jameson thanks Amy and heads to the upstairs bathroom. She is so flustered after the events of the past few days.

She notices she has no clean towels in her drawer. She heads towards the top of the stairs and yells, "Hey Am, are there any towels in your dresser? I'm out in my room."

Amy yells back up in response to her mom, and lets her know that there should be one or two of them on the coat rack near her bed. Mrs. Jameson goes into Amy's room, tripping over the overflowing basket of laundry. She reaches Amy's coat rack and grabs a towel. When she removes the towel from the rack she notices Amy's necklace. She is fairly certain this is the necklace that Amy was tricked into going to claim, when Spencer was attacked. This strikes Mrs. Jameson as odd. She did not think Amy ever actually received the necklace that day. She is also not certain it actually ever went missing in the first place. Mrs. Jameson doesn't have the luxury of ignoring any details or questions, given the recent events.

"Hey Amy!" her mom yells down and awaits a response.

"Yeah? Mom?"

Amy's mom asks if she can come upstairs and instantly hears Amy's footsteps bounding the steps.

Amy pushes the bedroom door open. "What is it? Is everything okay?"

"Yeah I think, but I was grabbing the towel and when I picked it up I saw your necklace under it... I thought that was weird because I didn't think you actually forgot it, or got it back that day at the funeral parlor."

Amy's eyes grow bigger and bigger and she loses her breath. Her mom sees the fear and curiosity in her daughter's eyes.

"That can't be here, mom. It can't," Amy says, tripping as she backs farther and farther away from it.

"Well, explain, sweetie! What do you mean?"

Amy takes a deep breath in an attempt to compose herself before responding. "I did lose it, or had it taken, or something. That's why it didn't seem suspicious when the parlor said they found it – at least, I thought it was the parlor. I never got it the day Spencer was attacked. It was all a ploy just to lure us there, mom... Someone put that here today – tonight, actually. It had to be when we were at the station or diner."

Amy and her mom are flooded with fear and uncertainty. They comprehend so little and they are uncertain if the intruder might still be in the house. They do a quick check of both floors and discover no one.

Mrs. Jameson asks whether this stalker is focusing on items to do with the keychain that Amy gave Kyle so many years ago. More importantly she asks why they are toying with the replica necklace Mark had made for her last summer. Mark knew how much the necklace meant to her – she had given it away years ago when she and Kyle still saw eye to eye. Mark had one made and given to her as a gift on her last birthday.

Amy has no idea where to even start with a response for her mom. She feels everything is closing in on her and she cannot protect her mom from the truth about the fire for much longer. If she does not come clean right now, she will not have any credible answers about why their stalker is focusing so much on Kyle and the necklace she gave him. She knows that if she does not explain it all to her mom then they will never be able to attempt to figure this out. Amy needs every ounce of help she can get, so she asks her mom to sit on the bed with her. She knows her entire relationship with her mom may change after this moment, but that is the least of her worries now.

She tells her everything. From the phone call to Spencer that night, to the blackmail she used to get Spencer to help her, and concludes with how Spencer drugged Kyle at the party that night. Mrs. Jameson goes ghost white from head to toe. She is in shock, so dazed she can't even muster up a tear or the slap in the face that Amy truly deserves.

"Mom... say something, anything," Amy mumbles as she continues balling her eyes out on her bed sheet.

Mrs. Jameson slowly sits up off the bed, and prepares to leave the room. "The only thing I will say is that your brother was the only person who was wronged in all this. Everything he said and felt about you was the truth... I knew I had a bastard for a husband, but never once did I think I raised a soulless bitch for a daughter. Leave me alone Amy." She slowly walks out of the room and closes the bathroom door behind her.

Amy lets out an uncontrollable wail as she continues to bury her face in her pillows. "I didn't mean for it to be this way, Mom! I swear!" she screams as she continues to sniffle and cry.

Her mom doesn't respond. Amy hears the shower turn on. Oddly, it never sounded more peaceful...

Chapter VI

Break-up gone wrong

The following morning, Amy awakes exactly where she was when she told her mom the truth. She is in a daze and a bit confused. Last night she did not get ready for bed or even brush her teeth. She cried herself to sleep and did not even realize it. She changes out of her clothes from yesterday, brushes her teeth and slowly makes her way downstairs.

Halfway down, she shouts out in a fearful tone, "Mom... are you here?"

She is disgusted with herself. Until last night, she never truly had to come to terms with what she and Spencer did. She had been burying it away, putting all the blame on this stalker. She now realizes that there would not be a stalker if it was not for her. She cannot blame her mom for reacting the way she did.

Amy reaches the bottom of the steps and turns the corner towards the kitchen. As soon as she catches sight of her mom she has to struggle to hold back her tears. Knowing how much she hurt her mom and how angry she made her is too much for Amy to bear right now. She approached the table, walking so quietly that she isn't sure if her mom hears her coming.

"I'm dumb, not deaf Amy," her mom says calmly.

"You're not dumb, Mom." Amy says.

"Well my husband had multiple girlfriends, my daughter lied about what she did to my son, and I had no idea about any of it." Mrs. Jameson says without looking up from her bowl. "I'd say I'm pretty slow."

Amy senses that nothing had changed since last night. She tells her mom again that she is sorry, but she doesn't know what else to say.

"I know exactly what to say. If you get hurt, I'll be by your bedside. If the police need us, I will also be there, because I am your mother and Kyle was my son. Other than that, any other personal relationship we once had is done."

Amy is blown away by this pronouncement, and hurt to the quick. She cannot believe this is what her relationship with her Mom has come to. She never imagined it could come to this.

"Okay, if that's how you feel then I can't change that. I go to college soon and then you'll be good. Can we talk about everything and at least try to solve it?" Amy asked.

Her mom agreed and continued to eat her cereal without looking at Amy. "So, tell me – what do you think happened with the keychain? I have nothing Amy. I'm lost."

On this point, Amy is as lost as her mother. She tells her mom that Mark is the only person she can think of who would know the significance of the necklace. He got her the replica for her birthday, knowing how much she missed the original she had given to Kyle.

"I don't need to spell it out for you," her mom says. "If what you say is true about the fire, and Mark is the only one who knew of the significance of the necklace, then he needs to be confronted."

Amy acknowledges that the point is valid. She goes to her laptop to check her messages. Ironically, Mark is calling her on Skype. She poufs up her hair even whilst trying to convince herself that she doesn't care what Mark thinks of her. Instantly she sees something is wrong. It is not Mark, and it is not someone Amy wishes to see.

The camera is zoomed in on a red lounge chair, in a dimly lit living room. In the chair sits Jenny.

Jenny has spoken to the police, and that was not in this stalker's plans. The killer did not take kindly to this development.

Jenny is bound to the lounge chair with a rope and sheets.

Amy screams for her mother, who heads over slowly, not understanding the severity of the situation.

"Mom! Fucking come here!" Amy shouts out in fear.

Her mom's eyes are now glued to the computer screen. The camera moves away from Jenny to focus on a small cage. Inside are two rabid-looking guard dogs. They itch, spit, and bite on the cage, doing anything to try to get free.

There is a look of death in the eyes of the dogs. The image focuses again on Jenny and the camera becomes still as though it has been set down. The next thing Amy hears is the sound of movement and the unlocking of the dog cage.

The two dogs fly into the frame. They treat Jenny's trapped body like a chew toy.

The color drains from Amy's and her mom's faces and their eyes open wide in terror. They both jump up to slam the laptop closed and fall back in their seats. Amy has a dead stare of defeat on her face. Then she leaps for her car keys and runs out the door.

Her mom – once again caring about her daughter's safety – shouts, "Amy, Am! What are you doing?" She continues to shout as she runs after Amy out the front door.

Amy is already in the car with the engine running. She yells, "I have to stop him!" and pulls out of the driveway. She drives out of the neighborhood in a blur, fumbling through her purse with one hand while steering with the other. Her makeup, keys, and pieces of paper fly around the front seat. She finally locates her phone and pulls it out of the purse.

Amy taps Mark's contact as she runs a red light.

She sees the green jeep coming from the side, about to smash into side of her car.

She throws the phone onto the floor so she can put both hands on the wheel. She turns right as hard as she can and hopes to avoid the collision, but the car veers wildly and teeters onto two wheels.

Amy's car and the jeep graze each other. Panting with relief, she makes her way safely down the next block. She picks up the phone again, forgetting she has already dialed Mark. She puts the phone to her ear and hears a single ring, and then it goes to voice mail. She throws her phone down in frustration and hops on the highway to get to Jenny's house.

Amy has taken the only car, so Mrs. Jameson calls the sheriff to inform him of the images they have just seen via webcam. She begs the sheriff and his deputies to get to Jenny's house as soon as possible.

Mrs. Jameson assumes that Jenny's time is up, but she cannot risk losing Amy, regardless of how angry she is at her.

"Winston you must stop by our house on your way," she says to the sheriff. "You don't understand – Amy took my car and sped off to Jenny's. I can't lose her too. Take me with you. You must."

Against Winston's better judgment, he capitulates. He tells her a squad car will be over momentarily. In the meantime, he will send deputies to Jenny's house.

Mrs. Jameson hangs up and runs to get her purse and put on her shoes. As she slides on her sandals by the front door, she sees the flashing light approaching their driveway. She rushes outside without shutting the door behind her.

She jumps into the back of the squad car with two deputies in front, and they speed off.

Amy arrives at Jenny's place. She pulls up with half of her SUV resting on the grass and half up on the driveway. She puts the car in park and runs out with the engine still running, racing toward the front door. The door is not locked, but it is shut.

She grabs her phone from her pocket and attempts to video chat Mark's account – the account that has been filming Jenny. It rings twice then goes black; a message on her screen reads, *user no longer online*.

Amy has had enough. She is infuriated with Mark due to their falling out. Now she is torn, attempting to grasp the thought that he might be responsible for all of this.

As scared and upset as Amy is, her only concern is to end this. Kyle did not deserve all of this. She wants to be at peace. After this life-changing epiphany, she opens the front door to Jenny's house and heads inside. All of the lights are off.

She heads past the entrance hall, passing the coat rack. She sees a glimmer of light shining from a room to her right. This seems to be the only light in the entire house.

Amy stops abruptly. She presses herself up against a wall. She realizes she he has no defense and no weapon of any sort. She feels her way a few feet to the kitchen and rifles through drawers, looking for a knife. All that she can find is a butter knife, but to Amy it feels like a 32-inch machete.

She walks back toward the lighted room. She sees the corner of the red lounge chair which she recognizes from the webcam stream.

"Jenny..." she says quietly as she inches closer and closer to the chair. "Jenny, it's Amy…"

She knows that Jenny most likely did not make it, or is no longer there. She finally reaches the side of the chair to see a pool of blood on the white carpet. Jenny's body is still bound to the chair, in the exact position she was in the video. Parts of Jenny's face are missing, and massive bites cover her from head to toe.

Trembling, Amy stares at this gruesome sight for a few seconds, and then falls to her knees and vomits beside the puddle of blood. She is crying uncontrollably. She is retching in agony for Jenny, and heartbroken at the thought of Mark doing all of this.

She sits up and leans against the wall. She is at a loss, emotionless, lifeless, and without a thought in her head. She is beaten emotionally and spiritually. She sits there, motionless, staring at Jenny. This is all her fault. She doesn't want to look but she can't help it. She feels responsible, and needs to see what she has caused by her selfish actions.

As she finally looks away, she sees something under the lounge chair, beyond the pool of blood. She tries to reach under the chair without disturbing the crime scene. She reaches around from the back of the chair to get what looks like old mail or pages of a magazine. She holds the papers under the lamp to see what they are. Fear rushes through her when she discovers this is another X-ray image.

The image shows the lower right part of a jaw, whereas the image Amy received in the mail was a shot of the skull from the side. She still has no clue what to make of this or why Mark might be showing her these images. What is the significance to Amy and what she did to Kyle? More importantly, why is Mark now determined to avenge Kyle, and what did he mean when he told Amy that Kyle was not as lonely as she thought? Amy can't begin to comprehend. She is utterly confused and desolate.

She flips the X-ray over to see if there is another note written for her, and sure enough there is. On the back of this X-ray is the message *she was seriously starting to annoy me*. But that is the part that strikes Amy's soul; it's what is under the message that makes her heart pound.

Beneath the message is a small image, scrawled in Jenny's blood. This design is a little like the cartoon Batman logo, but it isn't a bat. This is a small, simple bull's-head design... very similar to the keychain. Amy takes a long look at it, trying to ensure she is not imagining things as a result of the trauma. She feels dizzy, and the paper falls out of her hand as she passes out on the floor beside the lounge chair, landing in the puddle next to Jenny's body.

Blurry shapes of faces appear and Amy hears familiar voices. This is all she can make out as she starts to regain consciousness.

"I'm sure she's fine," Amy hears the sheriff's voice say to her mother. "We will run a psyche evaluation, but I'm sure it was just a lot for a girl her age to see."

They lay Amy on a couch. Her eyes are trained on the ceiling. The blurriness of her vision finally begins to fade as she slowly sits upright. She notices she has a burgeoning headache.

"Oh Amy," Mrs. Jameson says. "Oh sweetie, I'm so glad you're alright. If something would have happened to you, the way things were left between us... I—" Her tears choke her off.

Amy gets the picture. She and her mom share a warm hug.

Sheriff Winston walks back into his office and shuts the door. He has a new pot of coffee and hands Amy a cup, along with a few aspirin.

Amy takes a gulp of coffee and swallows the pills. "What happened? Did I get knocked out? Did Mark do this? Did you catch him?"

"Unfortunately, we don't know yet Amy. You are lucky to be alive. You passed out after discovering Jenny's body. Just rushing into a dangerous crime scene like that was not a wise idea. We have nothing to tie Mark to this yet, except for his web chat account being used to call you during Jenny's attack. Mark knowing the significance of the keychain is not enough to go on. It's just not concrete.

"The web broadcast could have been hacked," the sheriff continues. "Also, we have no idea where Mark is. We had deputies check his house. His friends have no idea either."

Mrs. Jameson interjects. "Well, is that not all the proof you need? When he finally needs to be questioned and found he is nowhere to be found! He's clearly hiding something."

Amy realizes how lucky she is to be alive, and starts to see that acting so rashly on impulse was a big mistake.

She accepts that she needs to be more rational if she wants to live to see Mark pay. She is determined to hear his reasoning for all of this, face to face.

"I understand," she says in a calm tone.

Mrs. Jameson turns to Amy with a quick jerk of her neck, at a loss for why she is not angry at the sheriff's nonchalant response to Mark's involvement. "Amy, we need answers, and no one here seems to be..."

Amy interrupts her. "Mom, fighting with Sheriff Winston will not help. He's right. Legally we do not have enough on Mark, regardless of how convinced we are that he is behind all of this. Sheriff Winston, do you have any information from the X-ray at

Jenny's house? That's the last thing I remember before waking up here."

Sheriff Winston informs Amy that he is running fingerprints on the X-ray, but has come up with nothing. "However, we did get a deeper look into the whole X-ray after the second note was left. The X-ray is of a male, though we can't determine the age, or the identity. It's just not possible unless we have a person to compare it to. Unless you can tell us who it is, or why Mark or whoever is leaving these, than we won't be able to identify them." the sheriff concludes dejectedly.

Amy and her mom share a look, both agreeing that there is no reason to inform the sheriff of the sad truth that Amy has confessed about the fire, though they never planned on sharing it with anyone; their family already looks bad enough.

"So, what is with this bloody bull logo next to the note?" the sheriff asks. "Your keychain is a bull or an ox, but what's the significance behind this, Amy? If you two want to end this and catch the bastard, you need to fill me in."

Amy elaborates on all the details, explaining how she ₅ this necklace from her grandma to Kyle as a Christmas present several years ago. She goes into detail about how much she loved it, and missed it, and explains that Mark had a replica made for her birthday.

She notes that this was the same necklace that went missing, and was used to trick Amy and Spencer into harm's way at the funeral home. She finishes up by explaining to the sheriff that when they returned home from the station the other day, her replica necklace was in her room on her dresser.

"That is all I can give you, I'm sorry. That is the entire story behind the keychain, and I do not know why it is being used as a symbol to torment me about what happened to Kyle." Amy says this with a guilty look, knowing Mark is trying to send her a message. He is using the bull as a symbol for Amy and Kyle's friendship, and he is doing so because he knows what Spencer and Amy did that night. Amy still cannot figure out why this affected Mark so deeply since he did not care much for Kyle. None of this information has been, or yed to the sheriff. Any feels that if anyone could get Mark it will be her.

. Jameson instructs Amy to get their purses and coats. Mrs. Jameson takes the sheriff aside in an attempt to be discrete. "Winston, do you think my husband is in danger? I mean, one of the women he was having an affair with has been killed, and he hasn't stopped by the house for any work files recently." Mrs. Jameson does not want to look weak, or to appear worried by showing she still cared about her husband's wellbeing.

Amy hears her but pretends not to.

"We know the hotel he is staying at," the sheriff replies. "I was going to go by later tonight to tell him about Jenny and ask him a few questions. We know he wouldn't harm Amy or Kyle this way, but he had relations with Jenny and then she ended up dead after their secret came out. I have to at least ask him the usual questions. I'll contact you afterwards and let you know he is alright, and we'll have a deputy stand guard outside of his hotel for a day or two."

Mrs. Jameson gently pats the sheriff's arm and thanks him.

128

Amy touches her mom's back and asks if she is ready to go. As they leave, they meet with a squad of deputies trying to push into the sheriff's office.

"Winston! Winston!" a deputy yells. "We got a hit on the credit card, we have to move out."

"What credit card?" Amy asks eagerly. "Who? Mark?"

Winston nods. "Yeah, it's him, ladies. We've had a trace on all his cards since we started looking for him. We just assumed he would never be dumb enough to use it if he was actually on the run."

Amy implores the sheriff to take her along, promising to do whatever he asks. Mrs. Jameson is not on board with this idea, due to the incident that just took place at Jenny's house. "No way Am. You just lucked out by passing out. This is their job now. Be patient."

Amy continues to plead with the sheriff to take her along.

Winston puts on his holster and grabs his jacket off the rack in the corner, without responding to Amy. Then he turns and says, "Your mother is right, Amy. If you are right and Mark is behind this, than this will be dangerous. Let us do our job and bring him in... If he doesn't give us a confession and cooperate we will let you speak with him, under careful supervision!"

Amy nods and reluctantly accepts his decision. Amy and her mom remove their jackets and sit to await the sheriff's return.

Winston heads out and jumps in the lead squad car. "Let's go. Move! Go!"

The fleet of police cars flies down the boulevard, only blocks away from the ATM where Mark's card was used. The ATM is located outside a Chinese restaurant on 6th Street. The sheriff's car pulls up first, followed by four others. The sheriff jumps out of the car before it even comes to a stop, and runs inside.

Only one or two customers are inside eating, so there is no crowd or activity for Mark to use as a diversion.

"Hello, hi, excuse me," the sheriff says. "Yes, have you seen this guy right here?" The sheriff holds up a picture of Mark.

Unfortunately, the employees do not speak much English. The cashier and the cooks look up in confusion, nodding their heads without comprehension.

Winston sees immediately that this is not going to work. "Where is your ATM?" he says, growing increasingly frustrated.

Frantically, and muttering rapidly in Chinese, the employees point to the right side of the building. Winston and his deputies go outside and approach the alley between the restaurant and a barber shop. Winston signals all the deputies to stop. They all load their pistols, and the three men in the back make sure their shotguns are loaded.

Winston inches toward the right side of the building. He presses his back against the stone wall and peers around the corner with his gun drawn. Three deputies turn the corner with the sheriff; without going any further. The rest wait for orders.

The sheriff spots a body beneath the ATM. Only half of the torso visible; the other half is under a bench. The man is face down, and is dressed in blue and yellow sweatpants and sweatshirt.

131

The sheriff slowly approaches the body. He can't tell if the individual is alive or not. He bends slowly with his gun still in his hand, to check the man's pulse. There is no heartbeat.

Winston sighs and hangs his head, disgusted that Mark has taken another innocent life on his watch. "Boys, he's gone. Go set up, call the coroner."

The squad of deputies leaves the alley. The sheriff remains bent beside the body, contemplating the horror of the situation. He finally decides to look at the man's face, to see if he knows the victim. He grabs a medical glove from his back pocket and puts it on. Gently, he pulls the man's shoulder.

The sheriff sees his face, and is filled with an overwhelming feeling of fright and confusion. This will change everything. Worst of all, the sheriff has no idea where to go from here. He is at a complete loss, and has not felt this away about a case in all his years in law enforcement.

The lifeless body is bruised, and has a bullet hole in the back of his head.

The man is Mark.

Beneath Mark's body is a five-dollar bill. The sheriff lifts it carefully and turns it over. Written on the back in blood is a message: *That's what he was worth.*

The sheriff sees now that another small bull logo has been painted on the side of the ATM. He pulls off the medical glove off, sets Mark's body back down, and punches the ATM as hard as he can. "God damn!"

The sound of crushing metal echoes throughout the alley, as a deputy runs over to check. "Sheriff, you okay?"

Winston turns to face the deputy and rubs his bruised, bleeding hand. "Of course I'm not okay! There's a goddamn psychotic wordsmith running free, and he's killing people all over my fucking town!"

Chapter VII

<u>Second Mistress</u>

The next morning, at roughly 8:45am, the doorbell of the Jameson house rings. Amy isn't sleeping well anymore, but her mom finds sleep to be the only thing that helps her. They are both extremely exhausted from the events of yesterday, but they still have not heard from the sheriff since he did not return to the station. Amy and her mom were instructed to leave with the promise that the sheriff would be in contact with them about what happened with Mark's credit card.

Since Amy is the only one awake, she goes to answer the door. Sheriff Winston stands on the doorstep, and Amy is certain he is waiting to share more bad news. In a time when it feels like nothing is going right, Amy is beginning to lose hope.

The sheriff is holding his hat in his hand, and brushes his hands through his sweaty hair. His eyes are swollen with dark circles beneath them.

"So, what's the word, sheriff?" Amy says.

The sheriff slowly eases past Amy and into the house. "Why don't we sit down? You may want to wake your mom up."

Amy demands that he tell her what has happened but the sheriff caution her to calm down and promises to tell her anything she wants to know. "Just wake up your mom," he says softly. "I'll make some coffee. It's okay, just go."

Amy rushes upstairs to get her mom out of bed. These days, that is not the easiest of tasks. It doesn't help that there are often two or three empty wine bottles on her mom's bedside table.

She pulls up the shades up, dispelling the cave-like atmosphere and allowing the sunlight to shine in.

The rays strike Mrs. Jameson's eyes like arrows. "What are you doing?" she mumbles in aggravation. "It's Saturday, Amy. Leave me alone."

"Too bad," Amy replies. "Sheriff Winston is downstairs and he will not give me an update on Mark until we both go downstairs, so please just get the hell up."

Mrs. Jameson has drunk so much, and was in such a deep sleep, that she has forgotten they are awaiting news from Sheriff Winston.

This is the quickest Amy has seen her mom hop out of bed in a long time. She leaps to her feet and puts on her slippers. They both head back downstairs.

Sheriff Winston is on the phone with what sounds to be the coroner or a deputy. "No I haven't told them yet, I just got here."

"Haven't told us what, sheriff?" Mrs. Jameson asks in an angry tone.

The sheriff turns in shock, and quickly hangs up. Amy has a look of curiosity and worry on her face, whereas her mother's is still pure frustration.

"If you guys want to sit down, we could".

"No we're both fine," Mrs. Jameson says. "What is going on?"

Amy hasn't moved an inch. She eagerly awaits the sheriff's explanation.

"Alright... alright," Sheriff Winston says. "The ATM that gave us a hit for Mark's card was at the Chinese restaurant downtown, near 6th. When we got there – well, there's no easy way to say this, ladies. We found Mark's body lying by the ATM. There was another note and another bull logo, but no X-ray. Our guy played us good. He used Mark's card at the ATM right before dumping his body. He left the note on a five-dollar bill. I'm so sorry Amy, I know you two had split up, but I am truly sorry."

This is the first time that Amy does not visibly react to news of a murder. She stares blankly at Winston, devoid of tears, with no reaction.

A few seconds pass before the sheriff asks, "Amy… did you hear me? Mark didn't make it. I can set up some sessions with our staff psychiatrist if you want?"

Amy snaps out of her trance. "Yeah, I heard you, sheriff. Did he suffer? What happened to him? What did the message say?"

The sheriff informs Amy she did not need to hear all the specifics, clearly attempting to avoid that conversation.

Amy is having none of it. "Yes, I do need to know all the details. He may be my ex, and I know exactly what kind of guy he was. But he was still special to me. I'm beginning to become numb to these visits, Sheriff. I can handle it, but I must know."

Mrs. Jameson rubs Amy's back softly, without intervening in the conversation. She sees how broken Amy is, but she agrees that if she is going to be terrorized she deserves to know the details.

"Amy... No, he did not seem to have suffered much. He had a small stab wound in his ribs, but the kill shot was from a pistol to his forehead. The message only said, 'This is what he's worth' on the back of the bill. So now that we have no real suspects, you need to hear me, Amy. Whoever this is, is taunting you about Kyle's death, but they also want revenge for it. Did this person also dislike Mark? Does that criterion fit the description of anyone you can think of at all?"

Amy stares into the distance, taking all of this in. She explains that the only people who did not absolutely love Mark were Spencer, Kyle, and her dad, a little, none of whom are possible suspects.

"I gotta go. Thank you sheriff. I'll let you know if I learn anything." Amy rushes to grab her coat and keys.

Mrs. Jameson follows her around the house as she gathers her belongings. "Now where are you going Amy? It's not safe for you to go off playing detective like this!"

The sheriff agrees, but he also has no interest in getting in the middle of this mother-daughter debate.

"Winston, tell her she cannot go!" Mrs. Jameson yells.

The sheriff acts as if he does not hear her, and hums as he heads towards the pot of coffee.

"I'm just going to see Spencer," Amy says. "He got home from the hospital last night, and he doesn't know about any of this. Maybe he can help. I was planning to go check on him anyway."

Mrs. Jameson knows she cannot stop Amy from doing what she has set her mind on, and at a time like this she wouldn't even try to prevent her from visiting an injured friend. She hugs her tight and begs her to be careful. She also tells Amy that she must text her when she arrives, and when she leaves Spencer's house. Amy agrees, and kisses her mom on the cheek. She waves to the sheriff, who is still in the chair sipping his coffee, and exits the house.

Mrs. Jameson closes the door behind her, turns and holds her hands in the air to the sheriff, a gestured demand to know why he didn't insist that Amy stay.

The sheriff shrugs. "I have a daughter of my own to fight with. This one's all yours."

Mrs. Jameson rolls her eyes and joins him at the kitchen table.

Amy pulls up to Spencer's house and exits her car. She is happy and eager to see Spencer, which feels odd. She cannot remember the last time she felt happy, let alone happy to see Spencer. She appreciates the friendship that has formed with him through all of this. She prepares to apologize for blackmailing him into helping her that night. She obviously did not know how it would all turn out, but she felt she had to do it. Spencer almost lost his life for her. She knocks and waits to be let in.

A few seconds go by with no answer, so she knocks harder, yelling "Spencer! Mrs. Maxwell?"

There is still no answer. Then she hears Spencer's voice from his couch on the other side of the door. The doctors have told him that he is not supposed to move. "Go around back. It's open. My mom's at work."

Amy walks around back, goes through the kitchen and finds Spencer on the couch with his shirt off, and a massive bandage around his torso. A stain is seeping through his bandage.

"Jesus, Spence you need to change that bandage," Amy says. "It's ripping, and it's way too bloody,"

Spencer gets to his feet, grunting and making slow progress. Amy lunges to help him.

"Well, if you're so concerned you're welcome to help me change it," Spencer says sarcastically, "because I can't reach all the way around my back."

Amy grabs the tape, gloves, and scissors off the coffee table and begins to undo and rewrap his bandage. "I assume you heard about my dad, and Jenny, the mysterious lady with the limp..." she says.

"Yeah... I heard about the whole thing. I'm sorry, by the way. Not so much for Jenny, but for what happened between your mom and dad. Kyle probably didn't have the chance to tell you, but my parents also split earlier in the year."

Amy hadn't heard about his parent's separation. She tells Spencer how sorry she is, and how she understands what he must be feeling.

"Well, thanks Am. But yeah, it's just something you have to handle in your own way. There's no set way to handle this. You can figure it out eventually, but it's not supposed to be easy in the beginning. You'll be alright. Unfortunately, you, I, and basically anyone in town have a lot more to worry about right now." He pats Amy's leg as she finishes up his bandage.

He asks Amy to fill him in on anything and everything he has missed. He explains how he has heard the headlines, but has no clue where the investigation currently stands. He asks if they are closing in, or if the sheriff has any new ideas.

"Wait, did you tell anyone about the fire?" Amy says as she finishes Spencer's bandage. "That's why I came over, Spence. Well, I came to see you obviously, to find out how you are doing since you almost gave your life for mine. Thank you by the way; you never had to do any of that." She leans in and gives Spencer a hug,

"Ahhh – stitches, stitches!" Spencer whispers. "Love hurts."

Amy apologizes and chuckles. She gets back to filling Spencer in on how much has changed since she last saw him. "The day you were attacked I told Jamie and Connor about what happened. They were really struck with amazement, as I expected, but they were not hateful or angry. They were more sympathetic. I also had to tell my mom. If you were there you would understand. I couldn't keep it from her anymore. I have never seen her so angry and repulsed in her life. We are not okay with each other and I don't know if we ever will be. However, under the circumstances, we are there for each other right now. The sheriff doesn't know, nor do the police, and my mom has no intention of telling them, either. That would implicate you so terribly Spencer, and my mom is tired of our family being a joke."

Spencer takes all of this in, and is amazed by what has transpired since he was attacked. He was hoping for better news, since so much time has gone by since his attack.

He is frustrated, but not at Amy, just with the general situation. "So, basically, we are back to where we started at the funeral home that day? We have no idea about the necklace, and no idea who could possibly be Kyle's secret admirer or friend or whatever the fuck this person wants revenge for?"

Amy can relate to Spencer's feelings of frustration. "Well, not exactly, Spence. There is something you haven't heard yet. Like I said, I came here to also inform you of some things. The replica necklace that was missing, the one I thought the funeral home called about, or the stalker called about – that was returned to my bedroom one night. Before you ask how or by whom – I have no idea. It was the same night that my mom and I took Jenny into the police station, and officially cleared her."

Amy takes a breath before she continues. "Mark did get that for me, so my mom, and the sheriff and I assumed it was likely he is involved, especially since I left him because of how much stress Kyle's death has put on me. The stalker is now leaving pieces of X-rays of a human skull, with messages on the back, for me, my mom, or whoever. This psycho is also painting a little logo of my bull

145

keychain at each crime scene. So whoever it is knows a lot about Kyle and my past, and our relationship. Hence the reason we assumed we had to check on Mark."

Spencer's eyes grow wider, and he sits back on his couch, resting his hands on top of his head. "Well, I guess this guy upped his game since I sat on the bench... So what is going on with Mark? Did you guys find him? Did that asshole confess?"

Amy informs him that they did find Mark through his credit card at an ATM. Spencer's face lights up and she hesitates. Then she blurts it out, and explains that Mark's body was found at the ATM and the note was on a five-dollar bill this time, not an X-ray. She tells Spencer that the message read, *This is what he was worth,* and explains that she didn't know why there was no X-ray this time. She tells him that an X-ray was mailed to her house, and another was left beside Jenny's body.

Spencer never expected to hear all of this. Upon Amy's arrival he assumed there would be some progress, and he tended towards believing that Mark was guilty. His mind was a whirlpool of confusion and possibilities, but he was beyond lost. "So Amy, where do we go from here? I'm done waiting around waiting for our worthless police to do absolutely fucking nothing."

Amy asks what else they can do besides wait for clues or new evidence.

Spencer raises his voice in aggravation and tells Amy that as soon as he is fully healed, he will handle things. "Once I can move around again I'm getting Connor and Jamie's new boy, he looks pretty good in a fight. Then once we know who this is we will take him out ourselves. No one's going to send three high school kids to jail for a self-defense murder against this creep. I think Connor also mentioned that Zach used to hack the web for music due to his DJ experience. Maybe he can help in technical way."

A few months ago Amy would have done anything to talk Spencer out of this suicidal plan. Now the world has changed in her eyes; she is willing to do whatever it takes to put an end to all of this.

She thanks Spencer again, and finally apologizes for what she did to him the night of the fire. "I should have never blackmailed you like that. That mistake was ours, not yours alone. I'm the reason this is all happening."

Amy swipes a tear from her eye; Spencer notices it and hugs her, allowing her to rub it off on his shoulder. He agrees to the plan; he has felt equally as guilty as her since the night of the fire. He has no hard feelings toward Amy and knows how sad and sorry she is.

"This is on me as much as you now. We're in this together, Am." he says as she pulls away, smiling and wiping the last tear off her face.

The front door swings open, and the sound of rattling keys invades the silence of the room. Spencer and Amy turn to look at the front door. Raindrops sneak in as Spencer's mom runs in. She is followed by someone holding a newspaper over her head to keep her dry from the storm.

The man holding the newspaper pulls his coat off the top of his own head, revealing his face. The expression on Spencer's face is nervous and awkward, but the look on Amy's face is something no one has ever seen before. It looks as if Amy might explode, cry, and fall over all at once.

The man who is supporting Mrs. Maxwell as she enters her home is Amy's dad.

Chapter VIII

Goodbye to Old Friends, Hello to New

The door remains open with the two parents in the doorway, as the rain drips endlessly onto the wood floor. Not one person has moved an inch since the newcomers' arrival.

Mr. Jameson has not spoken to Amy since the night she discovered his affair or affairs. He is looking at her for her reaction, beyond frightened; he sees the look of betrayal in her eyes. Not only with Jenny, but with the fact he couldn't contain himself from pursuing her friend's mother either.

Amy is thinking exactly that and is unsure if Spencer is feeling the same way. What Amy does not know is that this is not the first time Spencer has seen their parents together. Spencer and his mom are having a silent conversation of their own. Mrs. Maxwell is wondering if he has ever told Amy. Meanwhile, Spencer is in utter shock due to having not warned Amy, and his not expecting the two of them to walk in anytime soon.

Amy is the one to break the silence at last. "Spencer, should I be worried that you don't look nearly as shocked as I do?"

Spencer sits up. He puts both a hand on each of her arms. "I did not know until two days ago; I found out in the hospital and heard her on the phone. I did not want to drop it on you after everything you just told me. Also, they already know how much I don't approve." He casts a death glare their parents' way.

Amy can see the honesty in Spencer, and she truly cannot even muster any amount of anger towards him. She knows how hypocritical it would be, she knows he must hate this.

She is not as understanding toward their parents. She grabs Spencer's hands, and holds them tightly for a split second. She assures him it is alright, and she knows it is not his fault. Spencer is extremely relieved, as he could not afford an estranged relationship with Amy, not now.

He stands behind Amy as she turns to her dad and Mrs. Maxwell. "So, was this also going on before, during your adventure with Jenny, Dad? Just cheating on Mom wasn't enough? You had to choose my friend's mother. Even worse – Mom's friend. Mrs. Maxwell, I just can't believe you – you are not who I thought you were."

She squeezes past her dad and Mrs. Maxwell, pushing them both against the wall. She does not even stop to put her jacket on, regardless of the torrential downpour.

Mr. Jameson kisses Mrs. Maxwell on the cheek quickly, and runs after Amy. Amy has no regard for the pelting hail. Her dad dropped the newspaper in the commotion. He also has no regard for the downpour. Amy reaches her poorly-parked car and attempts to grab her keys and unlock it before her dad reaches her, but fails. In her frenzy, Amy has grabbed the wrong key.

Without being rough, her dad grabs her and calms her down. She yells for him to let her go.

Spencer has been watching from the door, but now he approaches Mr. Jameson as quickly as he can, given his injury. Mr. Jameson sees Spencer getting closer. He lets Amy go and she calms down.

Spencer gives Mr. Jameson a look he does not want to ever receive again. Mr. Jameson interprets it as clear as crystal: "Touch her again, and you'll have bandages too."

Spencer's mom is frightened, having never seen Spencer like this in his whole life. All four of them now stand in the pouring rain.

Amy shouts out over the rumble of the hail, "What do you want to say? 'Sorry for cheating, again – oh, and sorry it was with our friends'? Leave me alone, I'm going home."

She jumps into her car and starts the ignition. Her window is down. Her dad leaps. As she struggles to get the car in reverse, her dad says, "This was never a thing until after I moved out, Amy." She does not see how it is relevant, or even an excuse.

Amy pulls the car back abruptly. She stares at her dad with a dead stare. She whips the car around a bit too quickly, hitting Mrs.

Maxwell's 'Welcome home' flowerpot. Then she proceeds down the road as if she merely ran over a penny.

Spencer is extremely relieved that Amy is not mad at him; that was his biggest worry. Already on top of this situation, Mr. Jameson makes his way back towards the door. Spencer and his mom are already inside. Spencer limps upstairs as fast as he can. His mom rolls her eyes and sighs, hugging Mr. Jameson. Spencer's bedroom door slams, echoing through all floors.

Amy pulls up her to house, thankful that the hail and rain have calmed. The skies are still a dull and foggy grey, which is uncommon in Gullburg after a storm. Usually a bright post-rain sky would shine, but this is not a typical time in this town. Many 'don't-ask, don't-tell' relationships and family secrets can be found in Gullburg, but never something a catastrophe as high caliber as this. The public have only seen the headlines and the obituaries. No one truly has an understanding of what is happening. Not that Amy or any of them do either, but the public had fewer details than them. To them this was just pointless, senseless murder with no motive. Having no purpose is what terrifies the public.

Amy sees no use in taking down her mom's spirits any further. She feels this is a secret that needs to be kept, for now.

Mrs. Jameson is not even home. Amy cannot think of any place she could be, seeing as how she rarely leaves her bedroom anymore. However, the car is gone and so is she. In fact, Amy is not concerned, as she has been hoping her mom would get out of the house.

Amy remembers she was supposed to meet Jamie and Zach for Connor's guidance counselor acceptance speech at the school. As usual Amy's mind has been preoccupied with horrible, newly-acquired knowledge. She really needs some social interaction. She leaves the house immediately so she won't be late.

She arrives just as everyone is about to sit down. The room is full; Jamie and Zach are standing at the back, against the wall.

Zach signals to Amy and points to where he and Jamie are standing. She waves back and makes her way through the crowd, squeezing along the aisles.

"Hey Am, how are you doing?" Jamie asks softly so as not to interrupt the speaker on stage.

Zach is feeling extremely uncomfortable, as is Jamie. This is the first they have seen Amy since the discovery of Mr. Jameson's affair. They also haven't had a chance to talk to Amy about Jenny's or Mark's murders. Jamie does not want to pry, and Zach feels he has no right to even open his mouth.

Amy responds in a whisper, "Been better, but it helps to get out, right?"

Jamie smiles warmly. She still is arguing with herself about whether she should bring up any of the new developments. She wants Amy to know she's there for her.

Amy can see her hesitation, and at this point can basically read her mind. "It's okay Jam," she says. "A lot of horrible shit has happened. I can't say I'm alright – it wouldn't be human to be alright after this. That's how I know this fucker doesn't think like a human. I know you care – just don't tiptoe around me. I can handle myself. No worries. I just wanted to be with you guys, to get my mind off it, for an hour or so, at least."

Jamie smiles back and they hug, shoving Zach to one side like a couch cushion.

"Yeah, we're happy you're here, Amy." Zach says as he loses his balance.

Amy pulls away and smiles. The sound of the microphone being turned on begins to echo throughout the auditorium. They all quite down as it is about to begin – Connor will soon speak.

Zach asked the girls in a confused tone, "What is this ceremony thing even for? I don't remember anything like this from when I went to high school."

Amy and Jamie chuckle. Jamie says, "That's probably because you weren't involved in student government…"

Zach cannot deny that, and he laughs. He did not like many extra-curricular activities. If an event didn't involve illegal music then it did not have his attention.

Connor is introduced by the principal as tonight's main speaker. He appears on the stage as the principal says, "Thank you all for coming today. This afternoon we are celebrating the newly-elected student body president. This individual will take office the start of next fall, after summer break. We have our current president, Connor Gregson here, to announce the winner and say a few words. So you can all stop listening to me – here is Mr. Gregson."

The principal claps along with the crowd, smiling as Connor takes the podium. Connor taps the microphone, sending another echo through the auditorium. He adjusts it to his height, and begins. "Thank you, Principal Mason. It means a lot for you, the students, and parents, to take time out of their day for this – to listen to me, your children's peer; it's a special feeling." He takes a long breath as he scans the crowd.

"I am happy to be here to introduce next year's student government president. Before we begin, I want to talk about some horrid events that have plagued our family. This is what we are, a family and school community. If we want to prevail, we need to let him, or them, know we are not afraid. We may be scared, and sad – but afraid, no. We are being treated like puppets, and right now the killer has all the strings. We need to cut them; cut them immediately. The killer does not control us; we do. Every loss, every tear, we grow stronger. If you ask me, that's more power than he will ever have."

The crowd claps, and cheers. Students, parents, and even younger siblings are touched by Connor's heartfelt message. It reminds everyone of the reason Connor was their president for four years, and he is going out like a great prophet.

Amy makes eye contact with Connor from the back of the room; they share a look of loving friendship. Jamie and Zach waved and smile simultaneously.

The crowd quiets down when Connor waves his hand in the air, signaling for silence. "Now, this night is not about me, or my speech. Tonight we are here to introduce next year's president of the Gullburg High student council. She is my very close friend, and I could not be happier to leave you with anyone else. I give you Sarah Gallagher. Congratulations!"

A young, tall, blonde girl appears from backstage. She is smiling from cheek to cheek, which are as red as the curtain behind the podium. Connor hugs her and kisses her on the cheek, then hands her his ID card for student council. The crowd instantly starts clapping, this time for young Sarah Gallagher. The principal approaches the podium to introduce Sarah, as Connor waves to the audience and heads backstage.

Connor hasn't given a speech in some time, so he heads directly for the water cooler near the equipment office. He finishes three disposable cups of water, and takes one more gulp as he turns to the office door.

"Easy crowd as always, huh Mac?" Connor says to the stage director in the office. "Killed it, didn't I?"

There is no response from Mac. Connor could have sworn he heard him, so he walks inside. There is a note on his chair, which is still spinning around. He must have just missed him. *Lunch time*, the note reads. Connor laughs.

He turns to leave, and is instantly nose-to-nose with an imposing figure wearing a massive papier-mâché mask that resembles an ox.

Connor gulps so hard he cannot snag another breath. The figure is dressed in black from head to toe. The mask is twice the size of a human head. Connor sees a heart-dropping, soul-shattering look in its black ox eyes.

Connor tries to back up and run away. The figure grabs his arm aggressively. After a struggle, Connor is handcuffed to the hook on the backstage wall. The masked figure puts a sock in his mouth and slowly backs up while watching Connor jab, pull, and kick to get free. He is unable to yell, and totally helpless.

The ox's eyes are staring him directly in his face as the figure slowly backs up towards the stage exit. He starts pulling the stage curtain open. This curtain is the only thing between Connor, the principal and the audience. It starts to ease open more and more; the audience can finally see Connor tied and unable to move.

The principal and Sarah see the audience's confusion; they turn and focus their attention on Connor restrained to the wall. Connor is the only one in view, but he is still able to see the masked figure in the far corner. He cannot warn anyone due to the gag in his mouth.

Connor's and the ox's eyes meet again. The figure slowly takes his hand off the curtain rope and grabs another string. Connor's eyes grow wide in confusion. He began hyperventilating.

Principal Mason leaves the podium to try to release Connor. The crowd remains gripped with fear.

The figure looks at Connor seconds before the principal reaches him. He pulls the string. Instantly, projectiles fly all over the stage and onto the principal's face, while Connor's body falls to the ground.

After shielding himself from the aggressive spatter the principal looks down at Connor.

Half of his face is missing. A mace ball from the scene room has been dropped on Connor from the platform above the stage. Half of the dull, fake, mace spikes in his cheek are up to his temple on the right side of his face.

Principal Mason falls to his knees, screaming in terror and hugging Connor's body. The audience members scramble, panicking, climbing over one another. Deputies instantly flooded the entrance hallway as pure mayhem engulfs the room.

Zach, who left to use the restroom after Connor's speech ended, steps into a side hallway to the right of the stage. He hears the commotion, but wonders what the cause could be. As he heads toward the lobby he hits what might as well be an invisible wall. As he turns the corner Zach is clothes-lined by the same masked man who killed Connor moments before.

Zach, lying prone, staring toward the ceiling, can make out a black-hooded, bull-masked shape above him. A hatchet pierces his side.

As Zach hears the roar of deputies running through the hallway toward him, his assailant turns and makes a quick escape, leaving Zach bleeding out on the floor.

Two of the deputies kneel to assist Zach, and the other two pursue his assailant. Zach is placed on a gurney and taken out to the main lobby.

Jamie and Amy are the first to realize that Zach is seriously hurt. They both run after the EMTs who are wheeling Zach out.

"Wait, wait, what happened?" Jamie yells as she rushes to Zach's aid.

An EMT holds her off as she attempts to get through to him. The EMT informs her that Zach needs to be taken to the hospital immediately, if there is to be any hope for him – of course, Amy understands. She turns to bury her face into Amy's chest, soaking her shirt with tears. Amy holds onto her tightly, knowing how Jamie feels.

"Okay, I'm going with Zach," Jamie says. "You must stay for Connor. One of us needs to be here."

Amy knows there is no arguing with Jamie. She hugs Jamie and wishes her luck, and then rushes back to the stage to find Connor's bleeding, lifeless body. She cannot bear to look, but feels a bit of relief as she sees that deputies have covered the body. She waits with the police, trying her best to help contacting his family members. The lobby clears, except for Amy and the deputies. Even the principal has left the auditorium; he is in shock and is being assisted by EMTs. The school building is as quiet as a ghost town. All have departed; some in shock, some fearful, and others terrorized.

As soon as Connor's parents arrive, their eyes meet Amy's. They walk toward her through the empty auditorium, the three of them embracing in a quiet, solemn hug. The hug goes on for what seems to be forever, as they know what Amy had been dealing with.

They feel for her even more now, as they see her suffer.

Chapter IX

Who to Trust?

Where else would everyone be convening but the emergency room? It's becoming a second home – one that none of them wished for, nor deserved. The only difference this time is that one of their loved ones has been taken from them. Connor's innocent life has been stolen in this psychotic rampage, which has no end game in sight.

Jamie is anxiously awaiting news, or to see Zach. The doctor takes him immediately to attempt stitches, and to prevent any more blood loss. Zach has lost a lot; the hatchet pierced a small artery. Jamie remains in the waiting room, clothes covered in dry blood from sitting with Zach on the ride to the hospital. The deputy, who followed, sits with Jamie and awaits news as well. He is also awaiting Sheriff Winston.

Sure enough, moments later, Sheriff Winston walks in, followed by three deputies. Amy has not yet arrived with Connor's parents.

The sheriff rushes in as fast as he can, and approaches the deputy sitting with Amy. He signals for him to get up and talk to him. Jamie does not take notice of this; she is still in a near-catatonic state.

"You're not going to believe this, Tony" Sheriff Winston says to his deputy. He asks Winston what is going on; he doesn't know if he should be relieved or terrified. This killer has established he can keep them on their toes.

"We took prints from all the kids in the school when the first victim was found in the janitor's closet. So we've been running those against everything in the auditorium, and we got a match, quick... The fingerprints on the mace ball and stage wire belong to Jamie Dunkin."

The deputy turns to see if Jamie has heard or noticed them. Sheriff Winston quickly grabs his arm and whispers angrily, "Don't startle her, you idiot. We aren't arresting her. We are going to follow her."

The nervous junior deputy nods his head, and puts his hat back on. The sheriff instructs him to go back over to Jamie as if nothing is wrong. He explains that he is to sit with her, and say that they were simply discussing the case.

"Once she sees her boyfriend and leaves, then we will track her and keep all eyes on her. Do not blow this, Tony," Winston says as he pulls up his belt and walks out the door.

The deputy sits beside Jamie again. She inquires him if he has any new information; she's determined to receive answers. The deputy does not know the extent of her knowledge or involvement in all of this. However, he is aware that it is his job to not let her know they are onto her. He feels conflicted at first; she seems torn up and miserable. He continues telling himself it is all an act, and that he should not feel pity for someone who might be responsible for this mayhem.

Abruptly, the doctor rushes through the doors to the waiting room. He does not look as if he is bearing horrible news, nor does he look ecstatic. He approaches Jamie and the deputy.

"The good news is that he is going to be fine," the doctor says cheerfully. "He's a strong one, and just has a few stitches. The bad news is that he does not have any insurance – and Zach didn't want me to mention this, but he cannot pay for this. Does he have any relatives who can help?"

The deputy looks at Jamie and waits for a response. Jamie informs them that Zach's parents live across the country, and do not speak to him often.

"Yeah, I know, I'll handle the payments," Jamie says "Just tell me what I need to do – but can I see him first, please?"

"Of course you can, come this way."

The doctor proceeds down the hallway, and Jamie and the deputy follow. They arrive in the A wing, where Zach's room is located. The door is shut as they approach and the nurse is still finishing up with the stitches. The doctor asks Tony if the police have any more information about what was going on, but the deputy has nothing that he can legally tell the doctor. Tony does not know if Jamie is aware they now suspect her. He has not given anything up yet.

The nurse leaves the room and the doctor allows Jamie and the deputy to enter. Jamie peers around the wall so that she can see Zach. He is in stable condition, resting in his bed.

"Zach! Baby, oh thank God. I didn't know what to think. This has been——"

Zach cuts her off with a kiss and a hug. He is elated to have survived and to see her again.

The deputy is hesitant to interrupt Zach's happiness, but he needs to keep the investigation moving. "Zach, I know this is all very recent, and you want to rest, but we need something to go on. Is there anything you can tell us about the person who did this? Did you see them? What did he or she look like?"

"Can any of this wait?" Jamie asks. "He's so pale, and he just got his stitches."

171

Zach sits up, grunting. "No Jamie, it's his job and I'm fine. We need to stop this from continuing, and I'm the only one who's seen him."

The deputy's eyes light up. "Him? You can verify it is a male?"

Zach's face takes a quick turn to disappointment. "Well, no. He had a mask on. I know it was a guy, though – he was too strong not to be."

The deputy agrees with that logic, but remains confused by what Winston told him about Jamie's fingerprints. "What do you mean by a mask? What was kind of mask? Can you describe it?"

Jamie holds Zach's hand and smiles as she waits for him to give a description.

"It was weird – I never saw something like this before." Zach grunts again, and sits up. "It wasn't even a mask. It was a Chinese-looking, papier-mâché design of an ox or bull. It was all so fast, and I could barely see him. I only made it out for a second."

Jamie hugs him, and asks the doctor and deputy if they are able to leave. The doctor approves Zach's release, but asks them to be patient while he gets Zach's pain medication and his antibiotic pills.

Tony also approves their release. However, his orders from Winston were that they should begin to monitor Jamie. Tony informs Zach he will have to either come to the station, or have a sketch artist come see him tomorrow.

Zach agrees, understanding the urgency. "It's only some stitches and I have pills. I'll come to you guys, don't worry."

The deputy pats him on the shoulder, and thanks him. "Alright. You rest up, and you two get home safe. We'll see you tomorrow." He informs the doctor that they are cleared to leave at any time, and then he exits the room.

Jamie gets the medication from the doctor, and signs Zach's release. She also handles the insurance paperwork. Jamie returns. The nurse has provided him with a wheel chair for release. Jamie takes over from the nurse, and wheels Zach out of the hospital.

173

Amy has just arrived at the opposite end of the hospital – the wing where the morgue is located – with Connor's parents. Connor's parents have barely made a sound other than their roars of endless crying. They haven't spoken a word to Amy yet. Amy knows they blame her for what has happened, and she feels worse than she has ever felt before. This time it is different. It is someone she has cared for, has known for years – this is someone's child. These are parents she has known for years. Amy can't imagine how they could not blame and hate her. She was not intending on being the first to speak; she is even hesitant to give a simple, "I'm so sorry." She and Connor's parents pass the lobby and enter the examination room, where Connor's body has been taken. It is still covered, and none of them are in a rush to unzip the bag.

Mrs. Gregson has yet to stop weeping. She approaches the table on which her son's body rests. Without letting go of her husband's hand, she inches closer and closer to Connor. Her husband's hands drops from hers as she approaches the table. Amy stands silently behind Connor's dad. It is as if she isn't even there.

Connor's mom finally starts to move her hand towards the zipper. Her hand is shaking uncontrollably. Her husband walks up behind her and puts his arms around her to hold her steady. Amy no longer has a clear vision of the bag or the table, and all she can hear is the zipper. It is the slowest and most abrasive sound she has ever heard. It is as if it is taking an hour to unzip, and Connor's mom has barely unzipped it halfway.

Mrs. Gregson lets out a cry. She can barely unzip the bag pat her son's nose before turning away. She falls into her husband's arms, soaking his jacket with her tears. Then she walks toward the door where Amy is still standing. She stops, as if she is going to hug her or exchange words.

"I hope you and your family are happy." she mumbles. Then she slaps Amy across the face with such force that Amy loses her balance.

Mrs. Gregson storms out of the room. Connor's father still stands there with his hand on the body bag. He watches Amy as she struggles to get back to her feet. Amy is in tears, and at this point wishes she could just sacrifice herself in Connor's place. Connor's dad leaves without saying a word. Amy slumps back to the floor, left alone with Connor's corpse.

Amy never imagined she could feel the way she does right now. She wishes she was on the table in Connor's place. At this moment Amy makes a decision: no one else will die for her. She leaves the hospital, wiping her tears and hiding the fresh welt on her cheek. She needs to go see Spencer; she is ready to handle this Spencer's way, the way he always wanted to. She is done with the cops. She doesn't know that Zach and Jamie have left, so she is unsure where they were. The hospital informs Amy that Zach was released.

Amy goes straight to the station before visiting Spencer. She assumes Jamie and Zach will be at the station; she is clueless to the fact that Jamie is under suspicion. Once she arrives there is no sight of either of them, or Sheriff Winston.

She asks the receptionist if she knows where Zach, Jamie, or the sheriff could be. The receptionist gives Amy no useful information, and tells her to take a seat and wait patiently. Winston comes out of the interrogation room and signals for Amy to join him. She grabs her bag and runs up to him, knocking over chairs in the process.

"Where are Zach and Jamie? Is he really okay?" Amy says, aware that she is ranting uncontrollably. "What is happening? Why is Jamie's car up on the TV in that room...?"

The sheriff insists that Amy quiets down, and come with him and that he'll gladly elaborate.

"Wait, what's on your face, Amy? Winston asks, pointing to the welt on her right cheek.

Amy's face becomes extremely red, a combination of embarrassment and sadness.

"Amy, this is something I can handle. Is someone hurting you?"

"It's not like that, I swear. When I accompanied Connor's parents to the hospital his mom showed me who she really blames for this." Amy wipes a few more tears away. "Honestly, I don't blame her. She's right. I'd switch places with Connor in a heartbeat. He didn't deserve this."

It is a rare occurrence for Winston to let his emotions show, but this is one of those rare times. He sees Amy completely broken and wishing her own life had been taken instead of others. He sees the sadness in her eyes. She has reached a level of despair where tears cannot even be produced. Winston brings Amy in close and hugs her. He even feels responsible at this point, and is equally disgusted with himself. He knows that he is going to have to fill Amy in about Jamie in a moment, but she is in no state of mind to hear that her best friend is behind this.

He pulls away. Nervously, he says, "Now Amy, you need to prepare yourself for what I am about to tell you."

Amy backs up slowly, scared and expecting the worst. She cannot think of one good reason why they might be tracking Jamie's car. Connor is dead, and Zach is now injured. She doesn't see why their focus was being wasted on Jamie.

"I'm fine, sheriff. I've had enough. Just tell me what the hell is going on."

Winston prepares himself for what may be a colossal heartbreak for Amy. "When the first attack occurred at your school, we fingerprinted most students. We recently got a match after Connor's attack. The prints were found on the mace and stage curtain. They are Jamie's... I'm sorry Amy, but there is no way we can ignore this."

Amy storms along the hallway, heading for the exit. Winston assumes she is on her way to go warn Jamie. She slaps his hand off of her shoulder, and continues on her way. This is exactly what Winston was afraid of, and he did not want to have to take this route. He does not chase after her. He lets her go; he is ready to radio to the security guards that they are not to let her out of the parking lot.

Amy has beaten the radio order. She has made it past the first layer of security, and has reached her car. However, they still have to buzz her out of the gate, and it seems she isn't going to make it past the final layer of security. She gets in her car and quickly starts the engine.

She speeds towards the gate. She is unaware that security is aware of the situation, and that she is not allowed to leave. The guards stand in front of the slowly closing, blinking gate. One waves his arms in the air, shouting, "Stop! Mrs. Jameson, stop! The gate will not stop. Orders are for it to be closed immediately!"

Amy pays no mind to the gate or the guards. There are only a few seconds left before the guards will become road kill. They dive out of the way, one knocking the other over as he dives into the security pavilion. Amy grits her teeth and hits the gas as she buckles her seatbelt.

She crashes into the gate at full speed, hoping to break through it. The gate explodes and smoke instantly shoots up into the air. The electric control box on the side goes up in flames.

Amy is knocked unconscious due to the collision, and she does not make her escape. Her car is stuck in the busted gate.

The security guards rush to the driver's side door, but it is jammed shut. One of the guards is searching the back seat for a crowbar or any tool he can use to crack the door open. He attempts to drag Amy out the back but her belt is jammed, constraining her inside the vehicle.

He runs to grab his baton out of the security pavilion.

"Fucking step on it, Jake!" the other security guard yells, while he continues his attempts to pull the door free.

The first guard finds the baton and throws it to his colleague. He smashes the window and reaches in to unlock the door. With seconds before the car appears ready to explode, he slices her belt with his knife. He begins dragging Amy's lifeless body away from the wreckage.

The explosion of the car shakes everything in a fifteen-foot radius. All three of them are knocked over, and the two security guards are now also unconscious.

Sheriff Winston and a squad of deputies run out the front door to douse the fire and bring them to safety. They get all three of them into the medical unit immediately.

"Sheriff, should I contact Amy's mom?" a deputy asks.

Sheriff tells the deputy to not worry about it. It is a call he feels he needs to make himself.

Chapter X

A Loved One Resurfaced

Amy has survived and the damage does not seem to be critical. She is being treated for severe concussion. The doctors are also working on getting some gravel and pieces of glass out of her side.

Winston called Amy's mom prior to them putting her in medical, and she arrived an hour or so ago. She is waiting in the guest room, which has a giant glass window to allow her to observe Amy. Amy's mom is full of nerves, crying, but is also thankful not to have lost her only remaining child. She starts to become impatient, but waits to be granted permission to go in and see her daughter.

Sheriff Winston comes back out of the interrogation room, where most of the deputies are still conducting the surveillance on Jamie.

"How could you let this happen? What the hell happened?" Mrs. Jameson shouts, pouting and repeatedly slaps Winston on the chest and face.

She is out of control and cannot be contained, but Winston understands her anger. He feels responsible, and has for some time now. Not just for Amy's injury, but for everything that has transpired.

Frantically, he tries to grab Mrs. Jameson's arms in a non-violent manner, as he attempts to calm her down. "Jess! Jess! Stop it now. This isn't going to help Amy. This is how she wants us to feel. She is breaking us, and we can't let that happen."

Mrs. Jameson's arms go limp as she falls into the sheriff's arms, continuing to cry.

"Wait, *she*?" Mrs. Jameson asks with a heart full of hope. "You're looking into someone new?"

"We have not caught anyone yet," the sheriff explains. "We made fingerprint matches, and that's what we're currently working on in there. We're tracking them and waiting for her to make a move."

Mrs. Jameson demands to know who it is, and why they will not let Amy leave. "Tell me why Amy wanted to leave so bad! Why can't she? Who the fuck are you guys tracking?"

He asks her to quiet down and step inside with him. He describes to her how and why they are looking into Jamie. Mrs. Jameson is just as hurt as she would have been if he were to have told her Amy was the killer. Jamie is like a second daughter to her, and has been Amy's friend her whole life.

"And that's why Amy was running? Was she trying to go see Jamie herself?" Mrs. Jameson asks.

"Yes. We believe so. We had to stop her, and we could not control this outcome. Amy took a risk to escape."

Mrs. Jameson is rushed with a flood of emotions. She cannot fathom why Jamie would be doing this. Jamie was the closest to Kyle, and Mrs. Jameson never thought she would want to make such a mockery of his death. She keeps thinking of one of the messages

185

the killer sent to Amy a while back: *Kyle was not as alone as you think*. She has no idea what to make of that. Thinking on it more and more now, she starts to form a theory. Jamie was always the one who gave Kyle the benefit of the doubt, and looked out for him. Mrs. Jameson starts to put piece after piece together in her head. She wonders if once Jamie found out Amy was responsible for Kyle's accident… she could have been so furious, that she did all this. Mrs. Jameson had no intention of telling the sheriff any of this, as she and Amy decided.

Since that is the case, she is relieved the police are looking into Jamie themselves. Now it all slowly starts to seem possible that Jamie may be responsible. It is painful, but possible.

"Well, what are you learning while tracking her?" she asks.

"We haven't seen anything yet. We could walk in there and arrest her for the fingerprints, but if she really is behind all this – which I find hard to believe – we only have one chance to take her by surprise. I assume she has someone helping her. That seems most likely, and this is also the best way to handle that scenario as well.

So, until she stops taking care of Zach, sitting inside, we will not take our eyes off of her." Winston shows Mrs. Jameson out of the interrogation room and into medical. "Amy should be awake, and ready to talk any moment. Go on in and wait. We have everything under control out here."

The nurse informs Mrs. Jameson that she is finishing up, and that she will be out of her way in a moment. The nurse then leaves. Mrs. Jameson slowly walks over to the bed, wiping tears from her eyes. She sees her daughter, all cut up and with bandages on her head.

Suddenly, it all hits Mrs. Jameson. Just a few months ago, she had a full and healthy family. It all seems like something out of a movie; she couldn't be more relieved that she still has Amy. She rubs Amy's forehead gently, and sits down next to her. "Sweetie, Amy, it's your mom."

Amy's weak and bruised eyelids start to twitch. She begins to open both eyes.

Everything is blurry. Her mom is just a blur to her at the moment. She still hears every word she said, though. "Mom? Where am I? What happened?" she asks in confusion. She has no recollection of the explosion.

"You don't remember anything, honey?" her mom asks. She fills a glass of water for her.

"I just— I think Sheriff Winston was trying to tell me Jamie was behind all this. Then it's just all black from there." Amy takes a sip of her water, "What was he talking about? Did you talk to him? That cannot be true."

Mrs. Jameson insists she takes a breath and calm herself. She sits down beside Amy. "Oh Amy, you ran out trying to warn Jamie. You tried breaking through the security gate when they stopped you. You could have been killed – what were you thinking?"

Amy sits up quickly and sets her water down. "I was thinking I needed to be loyal and warn Jamie that they were trying to pin this on her, because they can't solve this on their own."

Her mom makes sure she finishes her water, and hugs her as she explains what Winston had just told her. "Amy, this is not any easier for me. I watched Jamie grow up with you, but you have to realize she was very close with Kyle. She is one of the few who know what you did. I don't want to think Jamie is responsible for this either, but we don't have the luxury of ignoring DNA proof. We don't have the luxury of ignoring anything right now."

As much as Amy wants to argue on Jamie's behalf, she sees the point her mom is making. Amy asks her what they should do, and suggests that maybe she could talk to Jamie. Amy feels she is the one who can possibly get through to her.

Mrs. Jameson tells Amy that the police do not plan to spook Jamie, or even make an arrest, until they see her make a move of some sort.

Amy sits back in her bed and crosses her arms in frustration. "So I am just supposed to sit here in this bed and wait, or hope Jamie kills someone else? That hardly seems like a sensible plan." she says sarcastically.

Mrs. Jameson hugs her again and promises this will all be over soon. The lights in the room go dark; they can see the blinking emergency signals through the glass window.

The siren sounds, and abruptly the entire building appears to lose power. Amy and her mom look around, startled and concerned. They see deputies running up and down the hallway in panic. Amy asks what is going on; her mom goes outside to investigate. Mrs. Jameson approaches the door just as Winston comes in. Mrs. Jameson asks him what has happened.

"We don't know. Someone took out our power and communications, somehow. Once our backup power came on, Jamie was no longer in her house and her car was no longer outside the residence. We are moving out to trail her now. You two stay put. I have guards in and outside the station. They'll protect you. If Jamie is coming here, we will be ready for her."

Amy and her mom look at the sheriff speechless, their jaws wide open. Amy begs the sheriff not to hurt Jamie and asks him to just bring her in quietly. Winston tells her that is what he wants, but she may not give him that option.

"Now stay put. I'll be back soon," Winston says. "Also, Spencer and his father arrived right before we lost power. They are on their way up to see how you are doing."

Mrs. Jameson tells Amy they have no choice but to stay put. All they can do at this point is pray things end peacefully. "At least Spencer has come to see you – we will have some company. Everything is going to be alright."

Amy is without any energy, but joyous that Spencer has come by. Amy attempts to make a subtle joke, implying her mom should hit on Mr. Maxwell. She says this because she is well aware that Mrs. Maxwell and her father are now seeing each other. Mrs. Jameson still has no idea. Amy figures she can stir the pot in her mom's favor; she is out to anger her father at this point. Mrs. Jameson laughs at Amy's comment and blushes as Spencer and his dad enter the room.

Spencer rushes to the bed to greet Amy with flowers and a hug.

"Wow, flowers? Spencer Maxwell, who are you? Ha-ha." Amy says, giggling. "Really, thanks Spence. I love them. It means a lot."

Spencer smiles at Amy and her mom. Mrs. Jameson floods them both with thanks for visiting.

"Wait, so how did you even know about the accident?" Amy asks. "Well you texted me you were going to come over after leaving Connor's parents at the hospital, and then you never showed. I got worried. I called Sheriff Winston and he told me what happened."

Spencer takes a seat at Amy's side on the bed, while Mrs. Jameson and Mr. Maxwell catch up in the corner. They used to be very close, and have not seen each other since he left town.

"I didn't know you and your dad saw each other, or that you two were on speaking terms." Amy whispers to Spencer.

Spencer leans over to respond. "Yeah, we grab dinner together like once a month when my mom's out. Today just happened to be the day we met up. He was really worried when I told him what happened to you. Does your mom know about my mom and your dad? My dad has no idea."

Discreetly, Amy shakes her head. She looks up with a smile as her mom and Mr. Maxwell approach them.

Mr. Maxwell kisses Amy on the top of her head. "How are you doing, Amy? It sounded horrible the way Spencer described it. I'm so sorry for everything that is happening. I wish I could have been here for you and Spencer. With everything going on with Spencer's mom and me, I didn't want to complicate things any further."

Amy is touched by how concerned Mr. Maxwell is with what they have gone through. Even after everything he has been through with his job and his divorce, he is still putting the children and the town first. His words fill Amy with optimism that there may still be some good in people.

"You have nothing to apologize for, Mr. Maxwell – this has nothing to do with you. This is our issue, but it means so much you came, and that you feel that way. Thank you." Amy says. She reaches up hug him.

Spencer desperately needs to speak to Amy privately about something concerning his mom and her dad. He suggests that his dad and Amy's mom go get some coffee and food from the lunchroom. He insists. They ask Amy if she minds, which she certainly doesn't. She can tell Spencer is trying to get them out of the room for some reason. Amy's mom squeezes her hand and promises they'll be back soon. Spencer hugs his dad.

"Great seeing you, pal," Mr. Maxwell says. "I'm glad we got to have lunch today, but I really should get going. It's about a three hour drive home for me." He hugs him back, and says his goodbyes. The parents exit the room together.

"Well, that was easy." Spencer says, laughing.

"Right?" Amy replies. "It seemed like they couldn't wait to get out of here and talk. I can't complain though – they both deserve it. But what were you trying to tell me?

"Oh. Well my mom has not been home in like three nights. She usually disappears some nights when she is staying with your dad, but I am starting to think they skipped town together." Spencer says while pacing. "It's not like I care anymore, I just didn't know how you were going to feel about it."

Amy is taken aback for a moment. As angry as she is with her dad, she never thought he would actually leave her without so much as a word. She is starting to believe everything she has ever heard about him. She is doing her best to accept all of it.

"Well, they can do whatever the hell they want," she says aggressively. "I don't need him, and you don't need her. We have bigger things to worry about."

Spencer asks what Jamie's current status is, and if the police are going to arrest her. Amy informs him that they are just double checking on her whereabouts. She tells Spencer that the sheriff promised to do his best to bring her in peacefully if they do have to arrest her. Spencer knows just as well as Amy that there are still no guarantees. He rubs his eyes and punches the wall, nearly knocking half the paintings off of the wall.

"Spence, I know you're mad – I was too. Look where it got me! I'm unable to help, or even move. I am stuck sitting in this fucking hospital bed."

Spencer rubs his bruised knuckles, and takes a deep breath. "I know. I know, Amy, but Jamie? She's one of us! If this was one of our friends this whole time, I do not know why you would want her brought in peacefully. If she really did this I would shoot her myself."

Amy is in awe of his anger, but she feels similarly, deep down. She is just not ready to admit it to herself yet.

Amy is having a much more difficult time letting go of the person that she thought Jamie was. "I am praying it isn't her, but if it is then I agree. I could care less about her if she's truly guilty. I must hear it from her mouth, while I look directly into her eyes. After I receive that confirmation, they can shoot her – or I will."

Spencer asks Amy if they are supposed to sit there and wait for news, since that has not proven to be successful in the past. Amy doesn't have an answer for him. Despite how frustrating this all is, sitting and waiting is exactly what they have to do.

Sheriff Winston and his squad of officers pull up outside Jamie's block. They have arrived as fast as possible. The tracker on Jamie's car is still in place and active. She is roughly three blocks away, and has stopped.

They continue to where her car is located on their GPS, but are careful to stay out of sight. They see Jamie in the distance – it is foggy and the night sky is getting darker by the second. They see Jamie pull over and reach into someone's mailbox. She seems to be fishing around for something specific.

"Should we approach the target?" a deputy asks over the radio.

"Negative," Winston says. "Negative, we are to follow, not approach. I repeat, follow not approach."

The sheriff sees Jamie reveal a small envelope from the mailbox. She opens it and begins to write something down in her phone, and then she drives away.

The officers let her gain some distance so they do not divulge their position. Jamie is driving at a normal speed and does not seem to be aware they are tailing her, unless she is deliberately leading them on. That is what has Winston worried; it is becoming too easy of a tail. He feels in his gut that this is becoming far too good to be true. After a few more blocks, Jamie pulls over to an Italian restaurant that closed down last month. She gets out of her car while continuing to type on her phone, and enters the building.

"Should we take position around the perimeter of the building?" a member of the red team asks.

"Yes, go now," Winston responds. "Stay quiet, and do not engage until I give the go. Send your men."

The squads file out of the vans and begin to surround the building. Winston is leading the pack. Two other deputies remain in the surveillance vehicles to ensure Jamie doesn't escape. Three deputies surround the left side of the building, and another group covers the right side of the building.

They leave the front entrance unguarded; the officers in the van have that exit covered. Winston and two other men head to the back of the building. They are using infrared tracking to determine whether Jamie is alone in the building. It reveals that she is.

"Sheriff, we have positive confirmation that she is alone in the building, I repeat she is alone in the building."

Winston gives the order. "Alright guys, we have one chance and this is it. Do not fuck it up. On my go, the red team will come through the windows on the left. The blue team will do the same the right. I'll burst through the back door." Winston loads his gun. "Does everyone understand? Alright, three, two, one move! Move in!" he yells.

Windows are broken as several flash bang grenades are thrown through them. The red and blue teams come through the sides of the building. Smoke and blinding light from the grenades fill the room. You can barely see more than five feet in front of you.

Winston and the others bust through the back door and approach the middle of the room. They see Jamie and corner her as she stands completely frozen in the middle of the old restaurant. She is standing in front of an old chalk board that was used for the weekly schedules at the restaurant. Jamie is caught off guard and looks more confused than concerned about getting caught. The flash bangs have knocked her over, and she lies on the ground covering her ears. The squad approaches Jamie, flip her body over, and begin to cuff her.

"No! No! What are you doing?" Jamie shouts out. "Amy, where is Amy? He is about to make his move on her!"

They pay her no mind and continue to cuff her.

Winston stands over her. "Yeah, yeah. Save it, you crazy bitch. We got you. Amy is finally safe. You can cut the shit."

He looks over at the old chalkboard that Jamie was staring at. He never thought in a million years that he would discover a degree of evidence this incriminating. He studies the board up and down, truly in awe. There are implications on the board from side to side – everything that he needs. There are copies of the partial X-rays that were left at some of the crime scenes. The logo of the ox keychain is drawn at the top. There are photos of Amy, her dad, and Mrs. Maxwell's on the board. Winston is overwhelmed with the amount of anger and disgust contained on this board. He peers around it and discovers what will blow his mind the most. Behind the board is a small shrine to Kyle, with flowers, candles, and photos.

Jamie is still being held on the ground in restraints. Winston continues to pace as he investigates the area. "So miss, how do you explain all of this? You aren't responsible, huh? Amy's in danger? How do you figure that?"

"That's the thing!" Jamie shouts. "I can't tell you, or Amy will die. That's what he said!"

Winston stares at her in utter confusion. "What do you mean, that's what he said? What who said? Amy is in the police medical wing, and she could not be any safer." He signals the deputies to bring Jamie to her feet and escort her to the car. "Take her away. I've heard enough."

"No! No, stop!" Jamie shouts back to the sheriff as they drag her out of the building. "Let me see Amy. Show me she is safe, and then I will tell you! I just need to know she is alright. Please!"

The other officers ask Winston if he has any idea what she could be talking about. They also ask if he believes if there could be any truth to Jamie's claims.

He shakes his head in absolute disbelief. "Believe her? What is there to believe? We just found her in a textbook psychotic lair. Now she wants to get in the same room with Amy? No way in hell. Get her back to the station and set her up for interrogation. That's an order."

Chapter XI

4 CCs

The sheriff pulls back into the station, followed by both squad cars. Jamie is still ranting and raving about her story, and that is exactly what the officers take it as – a story. They are all confident that they have finally put an end to the madness. However, so many questions are still left unanswered. Why did she do it? Why was she filled with such rage? More importantly, what did these X-rays have to do with Amy and Kyle? Winston understands the mocking of the keychain, and the logos of the ox. That is the only part that seems to make sense to the sheriff.

They all enter the building and Sheriff Winston instructs the officers to go set Jamie up in interrogation. He tells them not to start until he arrives. Winston is going to inform Amy that they have caught Jamie red-handed. He goes back to medical and enters Amy's room. He is greeted by Mrs. Jameson, Amy and Spencer.

"Well folks, you can be at ease. We got her. Textbook."

"You're kidding! She confessed it was her?" Amy asks in disbelief.

"What happened?" Is Jamie hurt?" Spencer and Mrs. Jameson ask in unison.

"Not exactly, she is denying everything. However, she isn't hurt. Winston says while removing his hat and scratching his head. "However, she cannot deny this. Not after what we discovered when we apprehended her. It couldn't have been more incriminating. She had a full board with copies of every single thing that we discovered at each crime scene. She had the x-rays, pictures of Amy, Mr. Jameson, and Mrs. Maxwell. She even had a small shrine to Kyle nearby."

He puts his hat back on. "She hasn't stopped going on about how she had to be at that exact location, all to keep Amy safe. She is blowing mountains of smoke out of her ass, if you ask me. We will have answers soon. We will know why she did everything, and the significance of all the hints she left. She is being prepped for interrogation as we speak."

"Wait, my mom?" Spencer says in a panic. "Why my mom? Also, why Amy's dad? My mom has been gone for three nights now. Is she in danger?"

Amy jolts up in the bed. "Yeah, what does my dad have to do with this? We haven't seen him either. I don't see him much anymore, but there has to be an explanation for his picture being up there."

"Well, we will go look into that, and put an APB out for both of them," Winston says. "I'm sure they are safe. With Jamie in custody, I think everyone is finally safe.

"Let's hope so. When will you know more?" Mrs. Jameson asks.

"That is up to Jamie, and how long she wants to keep playing these games with us. Our interrogator is no rookie. We will get the answers out of her. I promise you that."

Amy asks about finally seeing Jamie to speak to her before all of this commences. Winston turns down the request immediately. He can see how upsetting this development is for all three of them. He offers a fair alternative. "If you truly want to watch this interrogation I can hook up a feed to the TV in here. I warn you, it may not be pleasant, but that is the most I can do."

Amy, Spencer, and her mom agree and request the feed is set up. They want to see this, and understand for themselves.

Winston leaves and an assistant comes in to set up the TV. Mrs. Jameson also leaves to use the bathroom. Spencer and Amy sit on the hospital bed together as the feed begins.

They see Jamie in the interrogation chair. She is handcuffed to the chair, with IVs in her right arm. Her face is full of fear. She mutters over and over, "I didn't do it! You can't do this! I was trying to save everyone. Stop!"

Amy and Spencer know how hard this will be to watch. This is someone they have cared about and known their whole lives.

Regardless of how necessary this is, and what she has done, they are not prepared for this agonizing sight.

The interrogator steps into the frame, accompanied by Winston. Winston began to speak. "Jamie. We do not want to do this, but you are not leaving us any option."

Jamie begins to shout again, "Look, I know how bad this seems. I can explain, but I cannot tell you guys! Those were his only rules. Please, you need to take my word. Please!"

Winston rubs his eyes. "Ugh, Jamie, you are not helping yourself here. Tell us why you did this. What are the X-rays, and why are you targeting Mr. Jameson and Mrs. Maxwell? Are they safe? Do you have help?"

Jamie continues to stick to the same story, and assures them that she has no idea why their pictures were on the board.

"Alright, Jamie. I am sorry you feel that way," Winston says. "Adam, give her two CCs."

Adam moves over to the IV unit and injects Jamie with two CCs of their highest performing interrogation drug. The station called it "f-x". The drug causes an individual to feel as if they are slowly drowning, but just to the point that they will never lose consciousness. Jamie shouts and shakes in the chair. Her shouts come to a halt and she starts to lose her breath. She is sweating profusely. Amy and Spencer can't bear to look at the TV screen much longer. They do not understand why she will not just cooperate and confess her sins.

Jamie continues to gasp for air, and attempts to rip her restraints from the chair. Roughly two minutes have gone by, and the dosage begins to wear off. She starts to get her breath back. The chair and her clothes are soaked with sweat. She is drained of all energy.

"Jamie, this is only going to get worse if you don't tell us what we want to know, NOW!"

"I... I don't know. I swear I have nothing to do with this," Jamie says, as tears flood her face.

"So tell me Jamie, why were you there?" Winston yells. "Why were all the clues there? Why would you ever be there?"

"I— I can't. I won't be responsible for Amy or anyone else getting hurt."

Winston rolls his eyes. "That's fine by me. Adam, give her another two CCS."

Adam heads over to the IV again, holding another dose.

Jamie starts shouting in fear once more. "No. No! Stop it!" she howls, before Adam is able to inject her. "Okay, okay! I'll explain! You must promise me Amy is safe. I'll talk, I'll talk – just make it stop!"

"She is fucking safe! She is in medical, and so is Spencer. Now help me understand why you did this," Winston demands.

"I did not do it! I got a text from a blocked number. It gave me an address to go to so I left my house and went. When I got there it was just a house." Jamie takes a much-needed deep breath, and wipes sweat from her forehead. "When I arrived I got another message, and it instructed me to go to check the mailbox. I looked inside and it was a note that had the address of the restaurant written on it. It also said I was to wait for further instructions or Amy and others would die. You have to believe me! That is exactly what happened. You can even check my phone. The note is in my purse. Check yourself!"

Winston is flooded with shock, amazement and, even worse, guilt. Part of him is hoping this is not true; he does not want to be responsible for putting Jamie through the agony she just experienced. Another part of him is hoping it is true, for Amy and everyone else's sake. They do not want to lose Jamie. He instructs Adam to get her water and an oxygen mask, but not to release her until he comes back.

He leaves the room and goes to look in evidence for her phone, and purse. He runs into Mrs. Jameson on her way back from the bathroom. She asks him how the interrogation was going, and he tells her what Jamie just told him. She waits in the hallway while Winston goes to check on the evidence.

Meanwhile, Amy and Spencer are still observing the live feed from medical. Both of them are at a loss for words. They can't believe that Jamie may be innocent, and underwent that hell to protect them. They are also distraught because if true, that means this is not over. It also means that both of their parents may be in danger. Amy and Spencer sit helplessly in medical, awaiting the consensus of the evidence search. The nurse brings in a tray of food for Amy, who has not eaten since before her accident. The nurse checks all of Amy's vitals, and leaves the tray. Spencer starts to cut the cheap and unappetizing steak as she is still very weak. He cuts the steak in half and he sees how raw and bloody it is. He shows it to Amy. They start to realize it is not blood after all.

There is writing on the plate under the food. Amy grabs the plate and tosses the rest of it in the trash to see what it says.

178 Jefferson Blvd. Business District. Show up and no more harm will come to anyone. How you get out of the station and arrive is your responsibility. You now have one hour. Think fast.

Amy and Spencer stare at each other in disbelief and fright. They have no idea how they could ever accomplish this task. There are deputies on every corner, and with the entire situation with Jamie, everyone is especially on edge. But they no longer need to wait for the evidence to confirm Jamie's story. This proves it.

Spencer knows that there is a window in the supply closet down the hall. He asks Amy if she thinks she can make it out the window. He fears she is still in too much pain. Despite the pain she is in, she knows she has no choice but to deal with it.

"Spencer you do not have to come with me," she says as she starts to get out of bed. "This is about me. He wants me and my family. You already got hurt and I am done putting other people at risk. A few months ago I may have accepted this offer, but that Amy was a selfish coward. I am done with who I was. I deserve whatever comes my way. You can't risk yourself for me anymore."

Spencer looks at Amy as though she has been speaking Indonesian. He smirks. "You must be really high off whatever they are filling your tubes with, girl, because I'm coming. I am driving, and we are finishing this." He tosses Amy her clothes. "You may be right, and he may only want you. But my mom is just as much at risk as your dad. I'm not sitting here while anything happens. I'll make a distraction for you to get to the closet. Then I will pull my car around and get you from the alley. Okay?"

"Alright, you're right. But thank you, Spence. I would have never made it this far without you. You also would have never been involved in this if it weren't for me."

Spencer nods, smiles back at her, and then heads out the door to distract the nurse. Amy starts to dress. She sees Spencer ask the nurse a question, and then she walks away with him. Amy rips the IV out of her arm. She peers around the doorway – there is no one in sight and the lights are still flickering due to the outage. She takes her chance and runs towards the closet.

She hears footsteps coming her way. She has nowhere to go. She looks in both directions and discovers a trash bin full of medical gowns.

She crawls inside and waits for the officers to pass. They walk past quickly. The coast now seems to be clear.

Amy jumps into the closet and closes the door. She opens the window, and sees that it is about a two-storey drop. Luckily there is a dumpster beneath, and she can hopefully fall to safety. She throws her bag out the window into the dumpster, and sees Spencer's car pull up right beside it.

Spencer looks up to see Amy freefalling into the dumpster. She lands on the dumpster full of trash bags, and hops out to safety. She is limping and Spencer can see that the jump hurt her.

She leaps into the passenger seat and Spencer speeds off. His car is skidding and sliding viciously as he makes the right turn onto the main road.

Chapter XII

Beneath the Surface

Winston comes back into the hallway where Mrs. Jameson is awaiting him. He confirms that everything Jamie told them was true. They are both so relieved – but now, once again, they have no suspects. They truly have no idea who could be the puppeteer behind these events. Winston heads back to interrogation to have Jamie released, and medically evaluated.

Mrs. Jameson goes back to Amy's room to tell her and Spencer the news. She arrives and sees an empty bed – and an empty room, for that matter. She is in a full-on panic and runs out immediately, shouting, "My daughter is gone, has anyone seen Amy? Anybody? Someone help me!"

No one is in sight at the medical wing; it is almost deserted. Mrs. Jameson runs back to interrogation to tell Winston that Amy and Spencer are gone. She flies through the door just as they are assisting Jamie to her feet. Mrs. Jameson holds Jamie's hand and tells her how brave she is, and expresses her gratitude for what she did for them.

Jamie is barely conscious but manages to smile, and musters up enough energy to say, "Don't let Amy get hurt, this will be for nothing," and instantly loses consciousness.

Winston comes back in, and Mrs. Jameson is still distraught. She tells him that they are gone. Winston instantly runs back out towards medical, followed by Mrs. Jameson. He sees the empty bed, and he immediately radios to all exits that they need to be on the lookout for Amy and Spencer.

The station goes into lockdown once again, but this time Amy has successfully escaped.

"Where could she have gone?" Mrs. Jameson says as tears flow down her cheeks. "Why would she do this, Winston? I can't lose her. I can't."

Winston assures her that will not happen. He searches Amy's room and sees the food splattered all over the floor. He picks up the plate, sees the address, and shows it to Mrs. Jameson.

"I guess we know where they are going," Winston says.

Mrs. Jameson starts crying even more, considering what the rest of the message says. "We need to get there. They cannot do this on their own. You have to save them."

"We are only about fifteen or twenty minutes behind them. We will handle this." Winston assures her, while he grabs his radio. "All units meet out front immediately. We are converging on the killer at 178 Jefferson Blvd. Business District. Amy and Spencer have snuck out, and are already on their way."

Winston hugs Mrs. Jameson and promises her he will bring them both back alive – and this maniac back in a body bag.

She trusts him, but is overwhelmed with stress. "Please, Winston. Please, she is all I have left!"

Winston assures her he will keep his word, and he runs out with the rest of the officers.

Their sirens sound and the block is lit up with the flashes of their lights. They speed off toward the business district, and attempt to acquire infrared on the building downtown. Winston realizes this is the hospital where Amy's father had his practice. There is no way this is a coincidence. This has to be the killer's final act. Winston fears that Mr. Jameson will already be there, or in the killer's possession.

At the same moment, Spencer and Amy arrive at the hospital. The building is seven levels tall, and they haven't a clue where to begin.

Amy receives a message as soon as they pull up: *The basement entrance. Come in alone, or your dad and Spencer's mom don't come out of this alive.*

Spencer is not on board with this request in the slightest. "Amy, I am not letting you go in there alone. No fucking way in hell. He is going to try to kill them, and you and I, anyway."

"Spence, I can't risk being the reason he kills them," Amy says, breathing deeply. "At least right now we have a chance to save them. You can find a different entrance, and try and sneak down into the basement. Track my location on your phone, and go from there. I just need to enter alone. Once I am in he will not be focused on you."

"Amy, I don't feel comfortab—"

Amy interrupts. "Spence! This is the only way. I let you come this far – it's my way now. It's the only way."

Spencer agrees, against his better judgment. "Alright… Just be careful, Amy. I am so sorry about everything that has happened. You will make it. I *need* you to make it. You are really the only friend I have left." He hugs Amy, refusing to let go.

"I'll make it, Spence. We will always have each other. Thank you… Thank you so much."

Amy runs down towards the parking garage where the basement entrance is located. Spencer pulls his car around the block.

He plans to make his entrance from a floor above and work his way down as discreetly as he can.

Amy reaches the bottom floor of the parking garage. There is not a single car in sight, but there is one truck that she recognizes. It belongs to the janitor. She figures the madman has probably already taken care of him. Without the janitor, there is no one else in the building. It is cold, and it feels as if no one has been in the hospital in days.

She gets another message on her phone: *Good, you actually can follow directions. Go through the door to your right. Enter the old autopsy office, and wait for me.*

Amy puts her phone away in her back pocket, and reaches for the sharp shard of glass she found in the dumpster. She hides it in her sock. She pushes open the door. This wing of the hotel has not been utilized for medical use or autopsy for years. The only thing in sight is a rusty old metal table, a flickering board where X-rays used to be studied, and a desk chair. She sees something on the board – she is sure it is a bunch of the partial X-rays this person had been sending her all along. She still has no idea what to make of it, but feels certain she will find out very soon.

She approaches the board and sees other documents hanging beside the X-rays. These are news articles that she has never seen before. She has no idea what they had to do with her, Kyle, or anyone for that matter. She gets closer to try and make more sense of them. *Breakthroughs in study towards AIDS cure. Dr. Jameson awarded for discovery of the century.* It all starts to come back to her now. Last year, Amy attended a ceremony during which her dad received all sorts of awards and prizes for this specific discovery. However, it still does not answer her questions as to why this is relevant, or who would care about it.

"What is this?" Amy whispers to herself.

The door through which she entered slams behind her. She jumps nearly a foot in the air and turns around. She is not alone anymore. She is finally face to face with her tormentor. Well, not so much face to face, more like creature to face.

There in the doorway stands a tall man dressed in doctors'
scrubs, wearing medical gloves and the same papier-mâché ox head
– the same man that attacked Zach. This is the first Amy has seen
this mask, and for once she is absolutely speechless.

"What are you...?" Amy asks.

The being stands still as stone, and leans his head to the left,
continuing to stare at her.

"Who are you? Why the hell are you doing this? What does
any of this mean?"

The being has yet to say a word. Finally, he starts to take
slow steps, inching across the room.

Amy backs up as much as she can, which is only a couple
inches until she reaches the wall containing the board. Her heartbeat
races and her hands perspire, to the point that they could not even
grip the shard of glass if she had to. The individual stops at the
midway point of the room, and stares at her with his pitch black
eyes.

He reaches out to the right and grabs the handle of one of the morgue refrigerator slabs. Slowly, he pulls it out. All Amy can see is a pair of feet. Dead or alive, Amy does not know.

He continues to pull it out further, and she can now see it is a living person. It is Mrs. Maxwell. She is tied up at the ankles and waist, and has duct tape over her mouth. Amy jolts, intending to run to her, but the individual holds his hand up, insisting she stops. Meanwhile, he reaches out with his other hand and pulls out another slab. This time, Amy can't bear to look; she is already aware of who will be on this slab. He pulls it out fully and, just as expected, it is her father.

Amy breaks down and falls to her knees, crying uncontrollably. "Dad! No! Why are you doing this to us? Who the fuck are you, and what did we do to you? What did Kyle mean to you? He had nothing to do with my dad's research!"

The man behind the ox head laughs. Amy cannot make out the voice from this laugh; this man is a total stranger to her.

He takes two more steps toward her, and begins to lift up the mask. "Oh, Amy. So confused, so gullible, and so fucking selfish. Just like your dad."

Just when Amy thinks she cannot be any more shocked, she is at even more of a loss for words.

"Mr. Maxwell…?" she stutters.

He sets Kyle's papier-mâché art project down on the table, and continues to laugh.

"Why?" Amy yells. "Why would you do this? You watched me grow up. You have known us forever. Our families were friends. Spencer is your son! Kyle was his best friend! What the fuck is wrong with you?"

"Oh, no. No, Amy. It isn't what's wrong with me. It's what is wrong with you, and your whole family, dear." He laughs again, and then says calmly, "You are right, of course – I have watched you grow up your whole life. I was able to watch you craft yourself from the sweet and caring little girl you once were, into the selfish, bitchy, whore that you are today. Just like your father."

"I don't understand… My dad and your wife were not even seeing each other until long after your divorce and absence from town," Amy says with absolutely no fear. "As for me... I have done nothing to you, or your family. You are just sick; you're a fucking sick person, Mr. Maxwell. It's ironic you chose a hospital because this is exactly where you belong."

"It is almost sad how little you know about your dad, Amy," Mr. Maxwell says, still laughing to himself. "But, since he and my lovely wife will be dead soon, the least I could do is walk you through this. I wouldn't want you to die before knowing. So today, class, we are learning about why stealing is wrong. Those medical articles you are curious about, those are what started this whole horrific chain reaction."

"You're jealous of my dad? That is your reason?" Amy's tone continues to fill with hatred and disgust. "He has money and you don't and that is why your marriage crumbled? That's your motive? That is pathetic."

"You never cease to amaze me, Amy. You truly fit the stereotype of pretty girls being the dumbest. I am not jealous of your dad, nor was I ever. He was my friend, and someone I thought I could trust!" He punches the defenseless Mr. Jameson in his chest. "Clearly that was not true. Those articles he wrote, all of his discoveries, and awards. All of that should be mine! I should still have a family, and I should be credited for the greatness."

Amy's face fills with confusion.

"You see, in my spare time I like to dabble in scientific writing. I noticed something very odd in one of my brother's X-rays one day. It was something a bit curious in his brain. Now I won't bore your idiotic self with the scientific specifics. The moral of this lesson is that I discovered the AIDS breakthrough. I wanted the publication and the recognition."

He throws his mask at his wife's face. "I figured what better way to do it than to ask my good friend here – your dad. He worked for one of the biggest hospitals. He had money, influence. It was perfect. So one day I decided to send him all my research and articles. I asked for some advice and if he could take it to his medical board for review."

Amy still stands defenseless at the end of the room.

"The money problems in my family were all but solved with these findings. Life was finally going to be good, but your father never took it to the board." He throws another punch at Mr. Jameson. "He felt it would be more beneficial to delete the emails from his inbox and the hospital servers. His smarty-pants self even found a way to delete them from my sent messages. At this point there was no proof, not enough to even launch an investigation. He stole all my work! All my dedication!"

Amy can't believe what she is hearing, but knows death is not the fair punishment.

Mr. Maxwell continues to rant, "Then the bastard decided to take credit for it himself, and claim all recognition and awards. Who would believe me? It was my word against his. That's a fucking joke."

He turns away from Amy for a second. She knows she needs to make a move, but has no idea how.

"So against my better judgment, I used the legal tools I had at my disposal though my office. They did not appreciate the heat brought by having a five-star hospital on your back. So, they fired me."

Amy's face flushes with amazement. She understands his anger, but it could never justify what he has done.

"I could not keep our family together, and she was disgusted with me," he yells, pointing at Mrs. Maxwell.

Amy is astounded by all of this and ashamed for her dad. She could not believe he would do such a thing. Well, a few months ago she wouldn't have been able to believe it. Now it all seems not so impossible anymore. She understands that every family has secrets, and that is normal. She realizes now that she truly had no idea who her dad really was, but that is okay with her. She knows who he was to her, and she loves him as a dad, regardless of who he truly was to others, and how he treated her mom. She could not hate him absolutely. He raised her, and treated her well her whole life. Amy almost feels bad for Mr. Maxwell, but it still gives him no right to take it as far as he did. It gives him no right to take other innocent lives.

"Look, I am sorry that all happened," Amy yells. "I'm sure my dad feels horrible as well. He could have never known it would have started a chain reaction this severe, that it would lead to your divorce. I know you, Mr. Maxwell – this is not you! Your mind is just twisted by anger and rage. There is still time to stop this. You do not have to do this!"

"You see, Amy, that's where you're wrong. I do. There is no going back for me, even if I cooperate and turn myself in; I will get the death penalty. I have dedicated myself to this, and it is what all of you selfish fucks deserve. So let's get on with it shall we?" he says while walking over to the controls of the morgue refrigerator.

"You still haven't told me why you would hurt Spencer, or why you started all of this when Kyle died," Amy says. "You owe me that – to look me in the eye and tell me the truth before you kill us."

"Fair enough. None of this accidentally started after Kyle's accident, Amy. Kyle's accident was far from an accident. I had been watching you kids for weeks before I started all of this. I figured an 'accidental warehouse fire' would make my job a lot easier."

Amy cannot believe what she is hearing. All this time she thought she and Spencer held all the blame for Kyle's accident, and a majority of it they did. She feels a weight has been lifted off her shoulders, only to be replaced with another.

"I was hoping to take you out in the fire as well, and maybe even Spencer. However, I am glad I didn't. I had so much more fun toying with you guys these past few months, between the X-rays and the logo of your keychain – the keychain that symbolized how close you and Kyle were."

Mr. Maxwell spits at Amy's feet. "That is why you also die – family is everything! You treated your brother like pure trash that you just throw away in the cafeteria. As for Spencer... He's my son and it was not easy, but he turned his back on me harder than his mom did! You think your dad and his mom really only started seeing each other after he left your mom? Yeah... that's what I thought. Amy, once again you are uninformed. She was in love with him for years – Spencer knew this for about a year. She asked him to not say anything and she would tell me when the time was right. He sat back, and watched, watching with her." Mr. Maxwell slaps his wife across the face.

"Spencer watched as I struggled to make money, succeed, and try to hold our family together – well, what I thought was my family. Once I left he had the choice to make amends, and move in with me. As you know, that is not the decision he chose." He gulps; Amy can see he is still deeply insulted by Spencer's actions. "He stayed in town with his slut of a mother, and around your family. You should hate him too – he acted as if he didn't know about your dad and his mom. He lied right to your face. At that point, he was no son of mine."

Amy stares at Mr. Maxwell in awe.

He looks up and blurts out in excitement, "Oh, this is the best part, Amy! You'll just love it. What better betrayal than to have my own wife clears my server, and delete all my emails to your dad. They worked my life like a puppet show. So now I'll end all of yours with a puppet show, and what a fun show it has been."

He starts to push both of the bodies back on their morgue slabs. Amy is at a loss for words once again, and remains in a daze and immobile. She feels lost, as if she in another dimension. She has all but given up. She doesn't know if she could truly trust anyone ever again. She is so angry with Spencer, but still she loves him as a friend. She is hoping any minute he will explode through the door with the police, and save her.

"So Amy, anything you want to say to daddy before he burns to a crisp?"

Amy's expression is a mixture of fright and confusion.

"Yeah, you heard right – burnt. It did not take much work, for someone as dedicated as me. A few small configuration changes, a blowtorch, and switch settings. These two morgue refrigerators are not meant to preserve bodies anymore, but to heat up to 300 degrees and cremate the bodies. So now would be the time to say something because the oven is almost done preheating."

Amy makes her move, and charges Mr. Maxwell as he turns to ignite the slabs. He had carelessly set his hatchet and pistol down on the table. She leaps over the table with the shard of glass in her hand – but he has been anticipating this. He turns around quick as a flash, and catches her arm with the blade in her hand. Her wrist is instantly twisted and broken. He then throws her over the table and continues with his plan.

"Ahh! No! DAD!" Amy shouts as Mr. Maxwell adjusts the final setting and both fridges begin to heat up. The screams coming from the inside of the slabs sound as if they have discovered hell. Both of them are ranting and shaking to break free. The screams echo in Amy's head even after they have stopped. Amy is in far too much pain, and can barely yell to her dad anymore. She just remains on the cold ground, crying and holding her arm.

Mr. Maxwell sits on the ground beside Amy. "Well, well, it's finally that time. I have been waiting to get rid of them and tell you all about this for so long. Doesn't it feel good? All that closure? I feel so alive, much more alive than those two pieces of charcoal in there."

"Well, jokes on you because Spencer probably told the cops where we are," Amy says as she continues to tear up. "He's been making his way down here this entire time. When he finds out this was you all along, I'd love to see you stop all the rage he will have."

"Oh that's cute Amy. You still think you both out-thought me again? I hate to break the news to you, but Spencer is not coming. In fact, he has been captured and tied up in a trunk for about twenty minutes now."

"No, you're lying," Amy shouts with all the strength she has left. "That's impossible. You couldn't have possibly done that, and still make it down here as fast as you did. You're a fucking liar."

"And the final surprise is revealed!" Mr. Maxwell says while letting his lips curl into a smile. "Honestly, Amy. Do you truly think with the kind of man your dad was, that I was the only one he wronged? Oh no, no, no. I could have never done this alone. There's a world of people who deserve to watch your dad burn the way I did. I have friends helping, powerful friends that you will never see, or suspect. It's much safer this way. Now if one of us ever dies, or gets caught – fingers crossed we don't – then this justice can live on. However, this all worked out perfectly, so I do not think they will ever be revealed."

Amy cannot believe what she is hearing. She had assumed she had seen and heard it all. This is a nightmare of a much higher caliber.

Mr. Maxwell stands and walks across the room to grab the shard of glass he had taken from her. "You will be dead. I'll handle Spencer, and maybe I'll give him a chance to redeem himself. I don't know yet, it depends how I feel in the morning. So, does that clear everything up?

Amy has no energy left in her bones. She looks to her left for anything to defend herself with: nothing. She looks to her right under the morgue slabs, and sees a sparkle underneath. She can't see exactly what it is; it may be an air vent. She quietly and carefully reaches underneath, attempting to make it out.

She cannot believe what she has discovered. She feels that she doesn't deserve to have someone from above looking after her. If she somehow survives, she plans to change her life. She is done being selfish. She owes it to everyone who suffered or lost their life to make life better for everyone around her in the future. She is praying she will get the chance to do so. In a way, she feels it has been Kyle protecting her this whole time. She knew she doesn't deserve it given how she betrayed him, but that is what was so great about Kyle. As much as Amy hated his opinions and actions, she knew that anything he did, he did to protect her.

She grabs the shiny and slightly rusty dissection tool from under the morgue slabs. She slips it up the sleeve of her uninjured arm. She closes her eyes, and goes back to looking weak and defenseless.

Mr. Maxwell starts to walk back towards her, holding the shard of glass. He kneels down over her, raises his arm and says, "Now you can apologize to Kyle in person."

Just as he starts to lunge the shard down towards her, she shoves the rusty tool in his right eye.

"Ahhhhh! Fuck! Fuck!" he howls. He drops the shard of glass and falls to the floor.

Amy slides away from him, and crawls over to the pistol on the table. Crawling and screaming, he comes after her. He manages to grab her ankles. She can barely reach the pistol, but stretches out as far as she can for it. She can almost reach it.

Out of his single working eye, Mr. Maxwell sees what she is reaching for. He grabs the shard of glass again, and stabs Amy in her ankle. Amy let out a piercing scream, then lifts her other foot up and kicks him in the nose with all her strength. He falls back onto his side and let's go of her ankle.

She crawls to the pistol and limps onto her feet. Blood is still gushing out of her ankle at a rapid pace. She points the pistol at him,

237

and backs up to the far end of the room. She stands shivering with trepidation. She can't maintain consciousness for much longer. Before she passes out, she reaches into her pocket and dials 911, and then accidentally hangs up.

"Oh, Amy," Mr. Maxwell says. He laughs even though he is in agony and bleeding everywhere. "What a fighter. This is so unexpected. Bravo, well done. Go ahead, pull that trigger. You want to do it."

"Hell no. I just dialed 911. They will track my location in seconds," Amy says with certainty. "Every officer in town is looking for us by now. That's if they aren't already on their way here. You aren't getting off that easy. You will be seen by everyone for what you are, and stand trial." She becomes dizzy. "After all of that, then you can die, or spend the rest of your sad life in jail."

"You see. That just does not work for me… I won't be in any trial."

Amy looks at him with uncertainty. It is as if he thinks she won't shoot him if she must, and she has no problem doing so.

"This is where the others who are helping me come into play. This won't be over, and you'll never see Spencer again. We took measures to make sure that this will live on until you pay."

Mr. Maxwell lifts the shard of glass, and slits his own throat.

He falls over face first and the shard of glass falls out of his lifeless hand. His blood is slowly pouring out on the floor, and onto Amy's shoes.

Amy drops the pistol. She cannot believe what she has just witnessed. She thought she won, and that this hell was finally about to cease. But that bastard still found a way to win.

She falls to the ground, unconscious before she hits the floor.

At this moment Winston and a dozen officers swarm the parking garage, and storm into the autopsy room. They look around at the bloodbath that has just commenced. Winston sees blood everywhere, and fears the worst.

The walls, the bodies, and the morgue slabs are still at 300 degrees. The officers rush to turn them off, but Mr. Jameson and Mrs. Maxwell are long gone.

Winston rushes over to Amy to check her pulse. He has never been so relieved to feel a pulse in his entire life. He walks around the room slowly. "Mr. Maxwell… you son of a bitch. Good, rot in hell you piece of shit."

He lifts Amy up and begins to carry her outside to the ambulance. "I want this entire room covered. Do not miss a single piece of evidence. I want to know exactly what went down in this room. Bag everything on that X-ray board. If Amy has any memory loss or mental damage, I need to know what happened in here."

Winston continues out of the garage where the squad cars and ambulances are located. Mrs. Jameson is waiting out there as well, fearfully awaiting news. She is distraught. She is an emotional wreck and is full of tears. She sees Winston in the distance, walking out with a body, and says a prayer to herself that it isn't Amy. She sees that it is and almost breaks down, but then she hears Winston shout, "We have a live one! I need medical now! NOW! Hurry!"

Mrs. Jameson rips through the caution tape, and runs towards Winston. "Oh my God! Amy! Amy! What happened? Is she alright?"

Winston tells her that Amy will survive, but she must be taken to the hospital immediately. Mrs. Jameson kisses her daughter's forehead, rubs her face, and smiles.

Winston loads Amy into the back of the ambulance, and slams the door shut. He punches on the back of the bumper, "We're all set. Go! Go!" The ambulance drives away.

"Who did this?" Mrs. Jameson asks. "Did you catch them? What happened?"

"It was Mr. Maxwell... We do not know why yet. There are a lot of unanswered questions, and a lot of evidence to go over. We are hoping Amy will remember everything and be able to fill us in."

Mrs. Jameson can't believe he would do something like this. She feels beyond betrayed.

"There were two bodies cremated in there. We cannot identify the remains yet, but it is a safe bet that it was your husband and Mrs. Maxwell. Amy will have to help us out there too, along with the dental records."

Mrs. Jameson begins to cry, hiding her face in Winston's chest. She may have been furious with her husband, but she did not wish this on him.

She is relieved that Amy is alright, but she could not help but cry. These are tears of sorrow and joy. As far as she, Winston, and Gullburg are concerned, this is all over. They have no idea about what Mr. Maxwell told Amy about others being involved. Winston thinks it is that his throat was slit – there was no way Amy could have managed that, especially from the way their bodies were placed when they entered the room.

He assumes that Mr. Maxwell did not want to stand trial and spend the rest of his life in jail. Winston does not question that detail much, he is just glad it is over. He is overjoyed that monster is finally gone.

"Wait, where is Spencer?" Mrs. Jameson says. "He wasn't in there?"

"There has been no sign of him or his car yet. Hopefully Amy will be able to clear that up for us as well."

Mrs. Jameson thanks Winston and kisses him on the cheek, then hugs him with every ounce of her strength. Propellers sound as helicopters fly above the town, beginning the search for Spencer. The night sky has never looked so peaceful to both of them. They know that they have made it. They are survivors in a game of madness, which they once viewed as unwinnable...

Chapter XIII

Misery Ended, or Continued?

7 hours later, 8:15am

The sun rises and the town feels peaceful for the first time in months. Everyone is back at the station, where Amy has just woken up. Her eyes flicker repeatedly as she comes back to consciousness. The first blurry visions she see are her mom, the sheriff, and Jamie sitting in chairs around her bed.

"Amy… Amy, can you hear me?" Mrs. Jameson asks. She leans in to cover Amy with kisses.

"Yeah… Yes, where am I?" Amy asks in a soft voice.

"You're safe, sweetie. You're back at the station. You made it. We did it."

Winston leans forward and rubs her shoulder. He expresses his gratitude for her bravery at the hospital. "Amy, I know you are very groggy and probably a bit confused. Do you remember everything?" he asks in a rush. "All we know is that Mr. Maxwell was responsible. None of the other clues make any sense. What are the X-rays? And what are the news articles? Why did he do it?"

"No, no. It's fine, I remember everything... He, he killed dad, and Spencer's mom..." Amy starts to tear up again.

"I know," her mom says while holding her hands. "I know, baby. It'll be okay. You made it. You did this, you saved everyone."

Amy takes a deep breath. "He told me everything, sheriff... I know it all. My dad apparently stole those research articles from him, and all the research. Mr. Maxwell sent them to him for advice and approval from the medical board. I guess my dad never went to them, and deleted the emails. He then apparently submitted them on his own behalf. In Mr. Maxwell's twisted mind this led to his poverty, and divorce. He was so sick, and so evil. He caused the fire at the warehouse. He mocked me with the ox logo and necklace, because he said I took my family for granted and didn't cherish

Kyle. All Mr. Maxwell wanted was a happy family, but he just snapped."

"So, all of this – it was his entire grudge against your dad, for cheating him out of fame and fortune?" Winston asks.

"Yes. All of this happened due to that single act. Wait – Spencer! Did you guys get him?" Amy asks nervously.

"No," Winston says. "We haven't seen him since he snuck out of here with you… We were hoping you knew where he was."

"Oh my God! No, you guys don't get it. This isn't over. Mr. Maxwell said that! He told me that he had help. He claimed more people were prepared to continue the plan if he were to die. This is not over. He said they have Spencer too. We need to find him!"

"Others? Who, sweetie?" Mrs. Jameson asks.

"Whoa whoa," Winston says. "Calm down, Amy. This case is finally closed! The town feels safe, and people are rejoicing. The last thing we are about to do is tell the public that there are other ox-headed psychos running around. I'm sure he just told you that to spook you before he killed himself. It was all he had left, to toy with your mind."

"No, that is not the case," Amy says, raising her weak voice. "Where's Spencer then? We can't just forget him and pretend he never existed!"

"Look Amy, I know you want closure for him. I do too. It is for the good of the town that this case remains closed. Mr. Maxwell may have even got to Spencer before he confronted you. Spencer may already be dead. I will look into his disappearance, but it will not be public knowledge."

"You mean it's for your own best interest?" Amy yells. "You don't care about what the town feels. You just want to be able to say you closed the case, and don't want another dead body to turn up on your watch. You're unbelievable. I will find Spencer myself."

"Now Amy," Mrs. Jameson says while brushing Amy's hair behind her ear. "Winston has done his best this entire time. Be considerate."

"Considerate? He is going to lie to the media and everyone in town. They need to know that there are still others out there planning to carry this on!"

"Think of me what you wish, Amy," Winston says. "I know you're upset, and want Spencer back. You can rant and rave to the media all you want, but it'll just end with you looking like the crazy one who cannot let things go. There is no way there are others. Hopefully I will find Spencer, but I think it's unlikely. It's most realistic that his dad did not leave that large of a loose end. I'm sorry, but this is what is best and this is over. We all need to start acting like it." He leaves the room to make his final statement to the press.

Amy is furious, and cannot believe how the sheriff plans to handle this. She sees Jamie across the room, waiting to talk to her. "Oh dear lord, Jamie, I'm so sorry about what they did to you. You should have never played along. You should have just told them what they wanted. It's on me that you didn't talk."

Jamie jumps on the hospital bed and hugs Amy like she never has before. This brings tears to both girls' eyes.

"Amy... It's okay," Jamie says. "I would never throw you to the wolves like that. I held out as long as I could. I am not the biggest fan of Winston after that, either. My mom wants me to press charges, but that is just too much. You're safe for now, and that is all that matters. If you truly believe there are others and Spencer is still out there, I will help you find him. Count on it."

Mrs. Jameson voices her concern, and tells them that they should consider listening to sheriff, and forget everything. "We are so fortunate to all be alive, and still have each other... Jamie, you didn't lose Zach. So much more will be lost, and so many more lives could be taken if we do not let this go. These 'others' may not go any further with this plan, even if there are any others."

"Mom – do you not believe me?" Amy asks feeling insulted.

"I do babe, I just can't handle anymore. It's not unreasonable to assume Spencer was attacked before his dad confronted you. It makes sense that Mr. Maxwell would say what he said to mess with you from beyond the grave."

Amy is livid, and can't believe that her mom is taking the sheriff's side. "Well if that's how you feel, you should go join Winston and the rest of the townies, out there at that bullshit press conference."

"Amy, stop – don't be this way," Mrs. Jameson says. "Don't push me away now, of all times. We have each other and we survived. Don't you realize how lucky we are?"

"Look, I love you mom, and always will. That doesn't change the fact that Spencer has risked his life for all of us since the day this all began. When I look for him, and discover who these others are, that won't change the fact that I love you."

Amy squeezes Jamie's hand. "If you aren't going to help Jamie and me, than that press conference is the place for you. We leave for college in a few weeks. I won't be living with you anymore anyway. This is my decision now. I am nineteen years old. I make my choices, no one else does. I owe it to Spencer, and I will find him. I do not deserve to be the one safe in this hospital bed, regardless that the fire was not an accident. I still am the reason Kyle could not get out."

Amy starts to lose her breath; the thought of Kyle helpless in the warehouse has her extremely shaken. "I have been a horrible sister over the past few years to him. Today is when I change that. I won't be who Mr. Maxwell says I am. Not for a minute longer. I will find him. Conversation over." With that, Amy turns away from her mom to face the window.

Mrs. Jameson loves Amy and wants her to remain safe. She understands where Amy is coming from, and admires her courage and this new heroic, honorable attitude she has acquired. This is not an Amy she recognizes, but she is proud of her. She has grown so much.

"Be careful..." Mrs. Jameson says. "I will always support you. You're right – I won't be at college with you. I can't stop you. I just hope you wise up and realize this is a bad idea. I am going to go and try to get us released. I love you so much. Just because I do not approve, does not mean I don't understand." She kisses Amy on the forehead, and then leaves the room.

Jamie and Amy hold hands and gaze out of the window, sharing a moment of peace. Both of them can feel it is not over, but this is the first moment of solace and peace they have both felt in a long time. They are going to cherish it.

"You know you don't have to help me, Jamie," Amy says. "Whoever these others are, they want me. Not you. They only came after you guys because you were close to me. It would be in your best interest to stay away from me next year."

Jamie looks at Amy as if she is insane. "You must be joking, right? Amy, you are my best friend. We have been friends our entire life. Zach is going to get an apartment on campus next year. He also won't be happy that they are not going to launch an investigation about Spencer. He will be on board quick."

"No. Not Zach too. I refuse to let you guys risk your lives for me anymore."

"Ugh. Amy, you do not have a choice. We love you. We are going to do this with or without you. We all stand a better chance if we do this together. So you can either try to find Spencer and discover who these others are alone, or with us. Regardless, Zach and I will be looking for Spencer."

Amy smiles, and begins to blush. "Zach must have such a hard time winning arguments with you Jamie." She laughs. "I can see I don't have a choice here. Thank you. I don't deserve friends like you two. Spencer deserves better too, but I am going to make this right. We are going to find him, and bring these other crazy assholes down as well. We just need to stick together." Her voice is full of determination.

"We can do this Amy, we will see Spencer again. Winston will be a laughing stock, and we will find these others. Mark my words."

"You're damn right, Jamie." Amy says. They continue looking out the window as the sun rises.

Mrs. Jameson walks back in with her purse, Amy's belongings and a wheelchair. "Are you girls all set?"

Amy and Jamie smile at each other, then both nod.

"We certainly are," Jamie says, still looking at Amy.

"Indeed we are, mom. I don't think we have been more ready for anything in our entire lives."

Mrs. Jameson and Jamie help Amy to her feet and into the wheelchair, and they leave the station. As they pass the press conference at the front, Winston and Amy's eyes meet – it feels to Amy as though it lasts years, but she knows it only lasts a few seconds. Winston can see the determination in Amy's eyes. He respects it, but is also worried for what is to come. Amy waves at him cheerfully, and they all file into Mrs. Jameson's car.

They drive home to have breakfast together. Amy knows deep down that this is only a temporary peace. She peers out the window and stares at the sky, while thinking of Spencer. "I'll find you Spence. You'll come home," she mutters to herself.

"What did you say, sweetie? You okay?" Mrs. Jameson asks.

"Oh, nothing. Yeah, I'm okay. For the first time in a while mom, I am okay. Everything will be alright soon. I know it..."

Mrs. Jameson's station wagon drives off into the distance. Amy feels warm inside, knowing her hometown will be safe. The danger wants her, and it will follow her. She couldn't be more relieved that she is leaving town. It is over for Gullburg, and its residents have made it. But it is far from over for Amy...

Epilogue

<u>Who Are They?</u>

Three weeks later, about one month until college move-in day.

Some time has passed, and Amy has healed from all of her injuries. There has been no suspect activity since Mr. Maxwell's suicide. She feels much more at ease, but still thinks of Spencer daily. She intends to start her investigation when she moves to school.

Amy comes downstairs on Friday morning to fetch the mail. She is waiting for her list of books that are required for her classes at Copenhagen University. She picks up the pile of letters and rifles through them quickly, seeing bills, church memos, and community flyers.

The last piece of mail has the Copenhagen crest in the top right-hand corner. She drops all of the other mail in her excitement, and rips that one open.

The message at the top reads: *Do you miss him yet? Good luck. Sincerely, Peter.*

She is confused; Amy turns it to the opposite side only to find a photo of Spencer, with the same message written again. He is bound by rope to a wooden chair, and he is sweaty, with bruises

covering his face…

R.I.P.

Kyle Jameson

Amy Jameson

Jamie Dunkin

Connor Gregson

Zach Austin

Sherif Winston

R.I.P.

Jenny Stockton

R.I.P.

Mark Moon

R.I.P.

Mrs. Maxwell

Anthony Maxwell

Mrs. Jameson

R.I.P.

Mr./Dr. Jameson

MISSING
Spencer Maxwell

48496028R00162

Made in the USA
Middletown, DE
19 September 2017